To my husband, Dave, who inspires all the best qualities in my heroes.

Chapter One

The last thing Lanie Phillips needed to hear was Christmas music.

She jabbed the button of her car radio and cut off a chorus of elves singing "The Most Wonderful Time of the Year." Wonderful? Not likely, considering she'd be spending it alone.

The wail of the wind intensified, and her headlights reflected off pellets of snow that whipped across her line of sight. She pulled her wool scarf higher around her neck. Even with the car's heat on high, the cold seeped in. She squinted through the squall of white, wishing for some indication that she was nearing the Mattox place. Finding her way down the county roads outside her hometown of Abundance, Missouri, was bad enough in the dark without adding a snowstorm into the mix.

Around the next bend, a small sign barely stuck out over the snow. "You're almost to the Mattox house!" it read.

She gave a silent cheer.

Hand-painted holly leaves and candy canes curled around the red and green lettering. Maybe Kelly, her boss, had been planning a big Christmas party. Whatever the reason for the sign, Lanie would take any help she could get to find the right house.

After another half mile, she rounded a curve and found a second sign: "Please park only on this side."

Kelly Mattox must have had some party in the works. Lanie could only imagine how flustered her boss must have been, canceling a party and leaving town unexpectedly.

Up ahead a mailbox read "Mattox" in reflective, stick-on letters.

"Finally." Lanie turned into a snow-covered gravel drive. To her right a small house sat close to the county road. Her destination was farther back, the two-story farmhouse at the end of the drive.

A tall figure jogged toward her, and the skin tightened at the base of Lanie's scalp. She had no intention of making the headlines. No plans to star in "Missouri Art Teacher Murdered While Pet-Sitting for Principal." She locked her doors and kept driving.

The figure waved, and a man's face, now illuminated by a flashlight, appeared near her window. He shouted something. Did he say her name?

Lanie eased to a stop and lowered her window.

"You're Lanie, right? Uncle Rich said you were coming." He reached out a hand in a large black glove. "I'm Kyle Mattox."

Oh. Her boss's nephew. He should be safe. And he sounded friendly, with a hint of the northeast in his voice. "Lanie Phillips. Pet-sitter." She stuck out a mittened hand.

He gave it an enthusiastic shake.

Kyle was tall and thin, from what she could tell under his bulky red ski jacket, and he had wavy brown hair and a narrow face. His mouth quirked to one side like he was on the verge of a chuckle, and his eyes were the color of dark-roast coffee. Lanie could see kindness in them and a resemblance to her boss.

She drew back her hand—perhaps a second later than she would have if she hadn't been staring at his knit cap. And its foot-long antlers.

This was her straight-laced principal's nephew?

"I live in the guest cottage with my daughter." He pointed to the small house at the end of the driveway. "I'm glad you're here to take care of Jellybean. My schedule won't let me be home enough."

Lanie glanced toward the cottage, then looked back at his cap and counted five jingle bells on each antler.

"Man, I bet Aunt Kelly gave you three pages of typed instructions." Kyle shook his head slightly, as if Kelly was lovable but a bit loony.

"Actually, it was four." Lanie couldn't keep the amusement out of her voice.

Kyle grinned. "She spoils that dog rotten."

Even though the chocolate lab was pregnant, Kelly had gone a little overboard. Lanie really didn't need all those instructions, as she had often helped her grandfather, a veterinarian, when she was younger.

She gave a rueful smile and moved a finger toward the power window button. The wind gusts were freezing, scattering snow over her face and the inside of her car.

"Daddy?" A young girl who looked like she was in kindergarten or first grade peeked out the back door of the cottage.

"I got it, April," he called back. Then he looked at Lanie. "I've been fixing one of the breakers. For the light show."

"Light show?" She released the control, leaving the window halfway up.

"Yeah, the Mattox Christmas Light Show. Since Uncle Rich has to be gone, I told him I could run it."

Judging from Kyle's tone, this was an honor akin to lighting the Christmas tree at Rockefeller Center.

"Didn't you notice the signs?" he asked. "People drive out to see it."

"They do?"

"Aunt Kelly didn't tell you?"

"Not a word."

If Kelly had mentioned it, Lanie would have stayed at her apartment and told her boss to find another pet-sitter. A bunch of cars going up and down the county road, honking at each other, did not sound like the perfect writing retreat Kelly had promised. But being somewhere different for the holidays, even just across town, had sounded good, like it might take her mind off things.

Because Christmas was wonderful, but . . . not always. Not six years ago. And not this year. Friends had invited her to spend the break with them, or just to come over for the big day, but she'd declined. She knew herself too well, knew she'd feel horribly awkward.

"April, hit that switch I showed you," Kyle called toward the girl. "We'll check the breaker."

Halfway up the drive, a trio of snowmen, each about eight feet tall and outlined in white lights, came alive and danced from side to side in rhythm to some unheard melody.

"Thought I'd fixed it." Kyle's voice held a note of pride.

"Oh, they're cute," Lanie said. Not worth driving seven miles out of town in the middle of winter to see, but festive.

"That's nothing." Kyle turned toward the cottage. "Flip the big switch, sweetheart," he yelled.

Behind him, eight reindeer began flashing, two by two. "Rudolph, the Red-Nosed Reindeer," performed by some '40s crooner, blasted from speakers in the yard.

Lanie cringed at the sound, then followed the flashing lights, glancing from the reindeer on one side of the drive to a ten-foot Santa on the other, as if watching an electronic tennis match.

"And that's just the beginning," Kyle said. "We have fourteen Christmas trees, sixty-two giant snowflakes, 'Happy Holidays' spelled out on the roof of the cottage, three more snowmen, and eight dancing gingerbread boys." He waved his arms, indicating features hidden by the darkness, listing each with emphasis, like a car salesman showing the top-of-the-line model. "Thousands of lights in the oak trees and—over by those pines—Mary, Joseph, and baby Jesus." He angled his head to point, and one of his antlers flopped over, making the bells jingle. "All lit with fifty thousand lights, activated in time to music on a fifteen-minute loop."

She stared, mouth dry, until "Rudolph" ended and Santa and the reindeer went dark. An off-key rendition of "Deck the Halls" screeched from the speakers. A circle of Christmas trees formed from lights and wire began flashing, one after another, in a pulsating, nauseating spiral, like some out-of-control carnival ride.

It was Christmas—bigger, louder, and tackier than Lanie had ever imagined. The antithesis of the holidays she was used to—tussling on the carpet with her nephews, sipping cocoa with her mom and sister, and watching her brother-in-law untangle all-white lights for a real tree.

Lanie turned back to Kyle and blinked, still seeing halos where her retinas spasmed from the lights. Even the first few notes of some holiday songs made her chest ache. And then there was the noise—the show completely short-circuited her plans for a peaceful winter break. How could she write while subjected to this?

"I did a bunch of rewiring last night to fix the sequences on those." Kyle waved toward the circle of Christmas trees. "I'll have to tell my new buddies in IT that it worked. Man, they are so jealous of this setup."

Lanie opened her mouth, then clamped it shut.

"I know, you hardly know what to say, it's so cool," Kyle said.

Lanie raised her window. The only way this would be cool was if the Mattoxes had a soundproof room in the back of the house. With blackout curtains.

Her back teeth pressed together, she gave a short wave and drove toward the farmhouse.

Kelly probably had her hands full watching her twin two-year-old grandsons while her pregnant daughter was in the hospital. Lanie didn't want to make things harder. She knew how medical issues could be overwhelming—she'd been there when Mom had gotten sick. But she had to finish her thesis before the break ended or she wouldn't be graduating.

She couldn't take the dog to her apartment.

And she couldn't work here.

First thing in the morning, she would send a text to her boss and gracefully bow out of this nightmare.

Surely Kelly could find some other dog lover who would appreciate Christmas on steroids.

ଓ

"I understand she texted you that she needs quiet," Kyle said into the phone. "But—"

Aunt Kelly interrupted him, explaining how important it was that Lanie finish her thesis, that there was no one else to watch Jellybean, and that the local kennel was out of the question.

Kyle held the phone between his ear and shoulder and wedged the last of the breakfast dishes in the dishwasher. Then he set a cardboard box on the kitchen table. He half listened to his aunt, more interested in unpacking. The compact, two-bedroom cottage would be plenty of room for him and April once the living room was no longer full of boxes. He ripped off the packing tape.

Kelly stopped for a breath, and Kyle jumped in before she could start again. "Did you talk to Uncle Rich?"

"No, but—"

Bits of muffled conversation between Kelly and Rich came through the phone line.

Kyle unpacked the toaster and some kitchen towels and broke the box down for recycling. Nineteen more to go. Moving, especially as a single dad, was not for wimps.

"I didn't realize you had already advertised the light show," Kelly said, back on the line with him. "But Lanie—"

April tugged on the leg of Kyle's jeans. "Somebody's at the—"

The doorbell rang.

"Got to go, Aunt Kelly." Kyle walked to the front door and glanced out the side window.

Jellybean stood on the porch, her head leaning against the leg of a blond woman.

The peeved pet-sitter from last night.

So the woman needed a quiet place to write.

So what?

Kyle had his own priorities. Like unpacking, getting up to speed at his new job at the hospital, settling April into childcare for winter break, and most of all, making sure his daughter had the best Christmas—and the coolest light show—ever. If it annoyed some pet-sitter or teacher or whatever she was, so be it. Kyle opened the door, ready to explain the facts of the situation.

"Hi. I wanted to talk with you about the light show." The woman sounded like it was the first item of business at a board meeting. He gestured for her to come in.

It had been so dark last night, he hadn't realized how striking Lanie was. Tall, probably almost five ten, with big blue eyes and honey-blond hair that fell past her shoulders, she wore a pink hat and scarf, gray mittens, and a coat the color of the Caribbean.

"I hope I didn't come over too early." She shifted Jellybean's leash from one hand to the other. Outside, the air stirred, and a faint scent of coconut blew in the doorway.

His mouth went dry. Suntan lotion. A beach. An image of her in a bikini. "Uh, no, I've been awake for hours."

April appeared at Jellybean's side and petted the dog's ears.

"Oh." Lanie's face softened and her tone became kinder. "Hello, I'm Lanie." She bent down and gave April a wide, relaxed smile.

"Hi. I'm April." She spoke with confidence, just like he'd taught her.

Kyle wanted to cheer. He'd worked hard to help April overcome her shyness, to teach her that she had to say a few words or people would think she was rude. It was paying off.

"Did you know Jellybean's going to have puppies?" April said quickly and edged closer to Lanie.

Kyle looked down at his daughter. The last time she'd said that many words to a stranger was . . . never.

"I did. I'm the art teacher at your aunt's school, but over winter break, I'm Jellybean's pet-sitter." She stood back up and gave the big chocolate lab a soft pat. "Now that I know what a sweetie Jellybean is, I wish I could have one of her puppies."

"Me too." April's brown eyes shone.

"April, why don't you go color in your room?" Kyle said.

"Can I show her my picture first? She's an art teacher." The awe in April's voice made it clear—art teacher was right up there with being a real, live princess. At least in April's book.

"Later."

"Another time," Lanie promised. "I really want to see your work."

April gathered her crayons from the kitchen table, then trudged down the hall, glancing back twice before disappearing into her bedroom.

Lanie looked at Kyle. "She's lovely. I hope I didn't wake up the whole house."

"It's just April and me," Kyle said. "I'm divorced."

"Oh." Lanie's voice was low. "Well, your daughter is adorable." Approval filled her big blue eyes.

Kyle stared. There was something about those eyes...

"So, I came to see what time the light show is." Lanie's businesslike tone was back. "Maybe I'm overreacting. It's only fifteen minutes and probably a couple nights a week—"

"Three hours, from six to nine, every night until Christmas. Starting Sunday."

Lanie's jaw grew tight, and she worried the end of the dog's leash between her fingers. "Oh. That is a problem. I'm on a deadline. I have to finish my master's thesis. And we only have a couple more days until Jellybean shouldn't be left alone."

"It's quiet all day here."

"But that's the whole evening, and I'm behind. With all I have to accomplish, I need every hour."

"Can you take Jellybean to your house?"

"Apartment. No pets."

Kyle thought for a moment. "The songs do get a little... repetitive. Could you try listening to some instrumental music to drown out the words?" There, he was being helpful. But he was not backing down. It wasn't his fault she was behind. The woman should plan better.

Color rose in her cheeks, and she twisted the leather leash handle back and forth. "Music distracts me—even instrumental."

A little weird. And again, not his fault. Not a reason to change the light show. "The schedule has already been in the paper. For a lot of families, this show is a highlight of their holiday. I can't cancel it now. It's a big deal, been running for decades."

"Could you turn it down?"

Kyle tried not to look at her like she was brainless. "People can't roll their windows down. It's too cold. Lots of folks bring the whole family, even babies."

"Your aunt said I'd have a quiet place to work." Lanie over-enunciated each word, as if he was the one who was an idiot.

"I just got off the phone with her. Things have been crazy, what with her flying down to Florida last week to be with my cousin Jill, and Uncle Rich heading down yesterday to spend Christmas there."

Lanie rolled her eyes, as if she already knew all about his cousin being in for observation.

Suddenly Kyle remembered where he'd seen those eyes, and his strong arguments dissolved into mumbling. "I, uh, think when Aunt Kelly talked with you, it was before I told Uncle Rich I could run the show. Before the ads ran. April and I only moved here a week ago."

Lanie twisted the leash handle further, until it began to double over on itself.

"Have you, um, considered earplugs?" he said.

"Earplugs?" Her voice jumped an octave. She unwound the leash handle and gave it a gentle tug. "C'mon, Jellybean." She spun on one heel. Gray pompoms bounced high on the back of her boots. "This is a waste of time."

Her boot heels clicked on the tile entryway and she stepped out the door, taking the scent of beaches and bikinis with her.

Kyle grabbed another packing box from the living room and set it on the kitchen table.

Lanie Phillips was not just some teacher who worked for his aunt.

She was Elaine Phillips.

He remembered those eyes from a photograph. One he'd looked at with a lot of unease. Even now his chest tightened, thinking about it.

If she was upset now, imagine what she'd be like if she knew who he was.

And what he knew.

Chapter Two

Lanie stormed through the living room, talking on her cell phone.

With the homey scent of a crackling wood fire and a chocolate lab who thought she was a lapdog, the old farmhouse should have been soothing.

It wasn't.

And neither was talking to her sister in California. Where was Megan's trademark righteous indignation when Lanie needed it?

"I bet the earplugs work," Megan said in a matter-of-fact tone. "Mark has a box of them for when he mows. I used some last winter when we were snowed in and I had to work at home with the boys."

"You haven't heard how loud the music is for this light show. And what if the earplugs don't work? I have to finish over Christmas. No more extensions."

"You'd think if the show was so important, one of us would have heard of it." Megan had a thoughtful note in her voice, and Lanie could picture her sister's face—eyes squinty, brow furrowed.

"Probably it's not important to anyone but Kyle." Lanie stabbed at the fire with a poker.

"But maybe," Megan drew the words out, "we lived so far out on the other side of town when we were kids that Mom didn't have the energy to take us after a long day at work."

"Could be." Mom did have her hands full, raising the two of them alone. "And these past few years maybe we were too wrapped up in our own family stuff." Lanie walked to the dining room and moved the centerpiece from the table to the sideboard. "Anyway, I'm sure people have better things to do these days."

"Maybe . . ." Megan said. "Tell me about this Kyle guy—"

"Later." Lanie cut her off. Megan wanted her to see every unattached man as a romantic opportunity. Lanie wasn't going there. She had no interest in being hurt, and that's what would happen if she dated again. Besides, Kyle might be cute in a geekoid kind of way, but look at how unreasonable he was about the light show, refusing to even turn down the volume on the music.

"I'm going to set up my work area and then give my boss a call. I probably didn't explain enough in my text. There has to be a way to curtail the noise."

In her classroom, a little noise, maybe even a little chaos, didn't bother her. Noise while working on her thesis was a whole different matter. She wasn't a bad writer, but she taught elementary art, not high school English. Coming up with six thesis chapters in ten days would be a challenge. Doing it while listening to the same fifteen minutes of music repeated for three straight hours, night after night? Her head might explode.

She fixed a mug of tea, set her laptop on the dining room table and plugged it in, then turned to glance at the grandfather clock by the baby grand piano in the living room. Plenty of time to call Kelly and accomplish a lot, even before lunch.

A soft knock came at the front door.

Lanie jumped up, startled. Today's plan did not allow time for interruptions.

She looked out the peephole.

No one.

She looked lower.

And saw a gap-toothed smile and a piece of paper clasped in a little purple mitten.

Lanie swallowed. She'd barely been home ten minutes. Not good, not good at all. She did not have time for a playmate.

But then she peeked out again at April's big brown eyes. Guilt settled onto her shoulders. The poor kid was probably lonely.

Lanie opened the door. She could take a quick look at April's picture, then say she was busy and send the girl home. So both she and her father would know that Lanie wasn't going to spend her break babysitting. "Hi, April—"

"I brought my picture to show you," April's words bubbled out. She held up her paper and gazed at Lanie.

Did April know how much her brown eyes tugged at a grown-up's heart?

Lanie opened the door wider.

Surely she could spare a few minutes. It could mean so much to the girl. Probably with someone like Kyle for a father, she didn't get much attention.

"I can't talk long, but I do want to see your picture," Lanie said. "Wipe your boots and bring it in the kitchen."

April stomped her boots on the doormat, then followed Lanie to the kitchen table.

Jellybean trailed along, stood beside April until she petted her, and then settled beside her with a loud snuffle.

Lanie sat down, ready to find something encouraging to say about the girl's art. Instead, she looked at it and felt delight blossom on her face. "Why, you've drawn Jellybean. And quite well. How old are you?"

April sat up taller. "Five."

"You've done a great job. Do you draw a lot?"

"Every day." Something in April's tone implied that anything less was unthinkable.

Lanie studied the little girl. Years ago, when her own dad had left, her mom had bought her a special box of colored pencils, a box she'd carried almost like a security blanket.

April looked down at the table. "I used to go home with my best friend, Suzi, after school and we'd draw at her house," she said. "And practice braiding our dolls' hair."

Lanie pointed to April's two braids, each ending in a pink ponytail holder. "Did you do these braids?"

"No-oo." April gave Lanie a look of incredulity, as if she'd asked if April could fly. "I can't do my own. Daddy did them. He studied on the Internet to learn how."

"Oh." Lanie covered a smile with her hand. There probably were videos on YouTube, but still, learning how to braid on the computer seemed silly. Then she pictured Kyle practicing on a wiggly five-year-old and her heart caught. A lot of dads would go with a ponytail. Or insist on short hair.

Maybe Kyle wasn't a jerk about everything. Just the light show.

"Uh, thanks for showing me your picture, April." Lanie stood up. "I'm afraid I have to work on my paper now."

April slid off her chair but didn't move toward the door. "I miss Suzi. I wish we hadn't moved to dumb old Missouri." Her voice faltered.

Lanie stopped and leaned back against the counter. No teacher could hear that voice and not recognize a child's cry for attention. Her thesis would have to wait. "Where did you live before?"

"In Chicago. Right next door to Suzi. But Daddy said the commute was too long and he didn't get to spend enough time with me." She let out a deep sigh. "I like having him home more, but Suzi's cat was going to have kittens."

"Well, puppies are nice too." Lanie waved a hand toward Jellybean.

"Yeah, but I don't think I'll get one. My dad says we're gone too long during the day." April's lower lip trembled. "And we won't be spending Christmas with Suzi and her family like we used to either. My cousins and aunt and uncle were supposed to be here, but they're all down in Florida. And grandma and grandpa are over in England. But Daddy is letting me help with the light show. I get to flip the big switch." Her face brightened. "Every night."

Guilt slithered off Lanie's shoulders and congealed into a gelatinous glob in her gut.

"That is special." She gave April's shoulders a squeeze, then walked her to the door. "What if you come by one evening next week, maybe Wednesday or

Thursday, and bring me the best picture you draw over the next few days? I'd love to see it."

"Okay." April plastered her whole body against Lanie, gave her a huge hug, then headed out the door.

Lanie watched as April ran toward home.

She thought she was so perceptive, and she'd been completely wrong. Kyle was only a jerk on the outside. Inside he was a big sweetie, trying to give his daughter a happy Christmas.

And she was being, well . . .

Awful.

If she called Kelly about stopping the light show, she would interfere with Kyle's efforts to ease April into a new town. She could at least give earplugs a try.

cz

April wasn't there.

But she'd been there. Coloring.

Kyle stood at her bedroom door, scanning the room. She had to be playing some game. But no fingers stuck out from under the frilly pink bedspread, no size-one feet wiggled among the little shoes in the bottom of the closet.

His heart beat faster and he dashed to his own bedroom and yanked open the closet door.

No April.

Sure, he'd been focused on unpacking, hauling empty boxes outside, but she couldn't have left the house without him noticing, could she?

"April?"

No answer.

The front door banged and he ran down the hall.

"Hi, Daddy." April walked to the hall closet, shoving mittens in her coat pockets.

"Where were you?" His words boomed out.

She flinched.

"I didn't mean to yell." Kyle lowered his voice. "But I couldn't find you. I thought you were coloring."

"I was visiting Miss Lanie."

Heat rose in his chest. "She should have called, told me where you were."

April stood on tiptoe to grab a hanger, her forehead wrinkled. "I don't think she knew that you didn't know."

Kyle slid an irritated glance toward the main house. The woman should have asked.

"Besides, you said that later I could show her my picture." April sounded like his concern was insulting.

He grimaced. He'd thought children didn't develop attitudes until they were in middle school.

Clearly he'd been uninformed.

He helped April put the hanger back on the rod. "From now on," he said, using the voice he reserved for when he had to be both parents at once, "no leaving the house without telling me, same rules as Chicago. Do you understand?"

"I understand." She sounded contrite. A little.

"And no dropping by Miss Lanie's unless you're invited."

"She already invited me over next week to show her another picture." April gave a nonchalant shrug. "She says I draw really well."

Kyle blew out a long breath.

Lanie Phillips was trouble. The worst kind.

Not only did she complain about the light show, but being around her made his brain fritz out. That coconut scent, that long, silky-looking hair. Add in the art factor and she was the worst possible neighbor. Some flake who would skip out and leave April feeling abandoned. Been there, done that. See the file marked "Ex-wife."

From now on, he and April would avoid Lanie. He'd make sure of it.

He stomped toward the kitchen, opened the fridge, and looked for lunch inspiration.

April tapped him on the back. "Daddy, Miss Lanie doesn't have one single decoration up for Christmas." She made the announcement in the grave tone normally reserved for discussions about reading, a subject Kyle still wasn't sure should be taught in kindergarten.

"She's only at Aunt Kelly and Uncle Rich's for a couple weeks, sweetheart. Probably didn't bring any." He pulled out some leftover pizza and set it on the counter. "And she might not celebrate Christmas. Some people don't, remember?"

"She wears a little gold cross on a chain right here." April touched her collarbone. "Like my Sunday School teacher back in Chicago. Didn't you notice?"

"Miss Lanie had on a coat when she was here." A blue one that matched her eyes.

"Oh. Well, I think we need to take her some decorations. Maybe one of those baby trees I saw at the store."

Kyle dug in the cabinet and found a can of sliced peaches. He was not going to buy the woman a Christmas tree. Definitely not part of the avoidance plan.

"Everyone should have a happy Christmas..." April's voice trailed off, as if she'd already given up hope for her own holiday.

Kyle's stomach tightened. He grabbed the can opener and cranked the handle, going around the lid bit by bit. He knew for a fact that six years ago Elaine Phillips had had a miserable Christmas.

She'd been thinking about china patterns and seating arrangements for a reception and, thanks to his good advice, her fiancé had left her.

Not at the altar.

Not quite.

Two weeks before the wedding.

So yeah, he knew about her misery then.

But that was no reason to take her Christmas decorations now. He—and most importantly April—needed to stay away. For their sake and for Lanie's. She had that thesis to write, after all.

"Pleeeeease. She's really nice, Daddy."

"Well—" Kyle dug the lid out from where it had sunk into the can of peaches. He would do just about anything to make April happy this Christmas. And something small for Lanie might help ease his conscience about the loud music. "All right."

April smiled so big that her cheeks rounded. "Thank you."

"But this is a one-time deal, like when we took some of your drawings to people at that nursing home in Chicago. Afterward, we need to let Miss Lanie write her thesis."

April's smile didn't fade a bit.

Chapter Three

This tree thing was a mistake.

In church the next morning, Kyle assured himself that it was simply a way to help April enjoy the holidays, that the fact that she wanted to do something nice for someone else was a good thing.

At the home improvement store, when he talked her down from the pricey tree that was already decorated, it still seemed fine.

But when April had babbled about delivering the foot-high artificial tree through lunch at Cassidy's Diner and all the way home, he knew. She was way too excited about Lanie.

And now he and April stood on the snow-covered front porch at Aunt Kelly and Uncle Rich's house.

The sky was an intense blue and sunlight brushed April's cheeks. She held the tree behind her back, her whole face strained, as if the excitement might overload her circuits.

"This is a one-time thing, remember?" Kyle said. "We give her the tree, a little holiday spirit, and then leave her alone to work."

April shrugged.

Might as well get it over with. Kyle knocked.

Inside, Jellybean woofed and footsteps neared.

Lanie opened the door, and the big dog squeezed past her to stand beside April.

"Hi." Lanie looked at Kyle with uncertainty. Her gaze slid down to April and she smiled.

"Hi, Miss Lanie." April said the words so fast that they ran together as one.

"Uh, hi." Kyle couldn't manage anything more. The smell of coconut seemed to bypass all logic, bumping up his heart rate and making it hard not to run his fingers through Lanie's hair, hard not to touch one finger to those lips to see if they were as soft as they looked.

"Are you still in your pajamas?" April asked with a giggle.

"April." Kyle silenced her. But the blue-and-green checked flannel pants and long-sleeved blue T-shirt did look like pajamas. Although she was wearing jewelry—the cross necklace April had mentioned.

"My pajamas," Lanie said in a stage whisper to April, "have bunnies on them."

April's shoulders scrunched up and she dissolved in laughter.

"This is a writing outfit," Lanie continued in a tone that implied everyone had one. "I've been working." She angled her head back toward the dining room. Kyle could see a laptop, a small printer, and a pile of wadded up pages. And hear the total silence from inside the house. How could the woman work without even the radio on?

April stood up taller. "Miss Lanie, they're doing a children's pageant at church." She sounded like she was looking for an advocate.

Kyle looked at Lanie and shook his head in a discreet no.

Lanie raised her eyebrows, then turned to April. "Pageants can be nice, but they do require a lot of effort. You might not have as much time for your art if you participate." Her voice was thoughtful, one adult woman advising another.

Kyle could have kissed her.

Uh, thanked her.

Whatever. She'd said the perfect thing.

"So, um, what brings you here today?" Lanie said.

April looked up at him and squirmed from side to side.

He nodded.

She pulled the tree out from behind her back and thrust it toward Lanie. "We brought you a Christmas tree."

"Oh, uh—" Lanie's face twisted as if she'd been offered the raw entrails of a Christmas turkey, then she dredged up a stiff smile. "Thanks."

She didn't sound the least bit grateful.

Kyle's chest tightened and he glared at her. Couldn't she see how much this meant to April? He should have known not to trust this woman.

"I know it doesn't have decorations, but I can help you make some."

He spun his head toward April. So that was why she had agreed to the cheaper, unadorned tree. "Sweetheart, I think Miss Lanie will want to decorate the tree herself, being an art teacher and all."

He put a hand on April's shoulder, ready to steer her back to the cottage. "We wanted to wish you a happy holiday and hope there's no hard feelings about the light show." He tried to sound sincere, in spite of Lanie's ingratitude. "But we know you have lots of work to do. We won't be bothering you." He gave April his best in-charge dad look. "Will we?"

April's eyes widened, then she shook her head a fraction of an inch.

"Merry Christmas," Kyle said.

"Merry Christmas. And thanks for the tree," Lanie said.

"Merry Christmas," April whispered, her shoulders drooping.

Kyle grabbed April's mittened hand and led her off the porch. It was a bit like pulling her away from the waterslide in the summer, but eventually she trudged beside him, head down.

He was doing the right thing, protecting his daughter, but in his mind two images alternated, a PowerPoint presentation with only two slides: April's long face with her sad brown eyes. And Lanie's expression when she saw the tree.

If she wore a cross, she was probably a Christian. And if she was, why did she look so upset about Christmas?

Was it all because of what had happened six years ago? That was far too long to mope around over a broken engagement. The guy had been a friend of a friend who filled a bedroom and paid his share of the rent after Kyle's buddy graduated early. And he was no prize. A woman as pretty as Lanie should have married somebody else by now.

Only she hadn't.

Kyle stomped snow from his boots and opened the door to the cottage. His plan to bring cheer to Lanie Phillips, and indirectly to his daughter, had been a total flop.

"Daddy?" April pulled off her wool cap and turned to face him. "If I can't spend time decorating with Miss Lanie, can I be in the pageant?"

No. Not the next week running back and forth to church every evening. Rushed dinners, delayed bedtimes, not enough time to do the reading practice the teacher had sent home for break. It was too much on top of unpacking, adjusting to a new job, and finishing his Christmas shopping.

"Please?" April hung on the word and peered up without blinking.

Kyle wavered.

"You said Christmas here would be even better than Chicago, but so far it's . . . not."

Ow. A direct hit. Kyle's chest ached like he'd been punched by a heavyweight champ. Not a forty-three-pound fairy princess.

He squared his shoulders and forced sincerity into his voice. "Being in the pageant is a great idea."

☙

Guilt and potato chips.

Lanie drove back to the farmhouse after a huge shopping trip. After today it would be too close to Jellybean's due date to leave her home alone, so Lanie had stocked up. All kinds of food, for her and for Jellybean.

Mostly, though, it seemed she was hauling guilt and potato chips.

The chips called to her from the trunk. It was past six, after all. Her plan to keep them for an emergency would require willpower.

As for the guilt, well, Lanie had tried Kyle's suggestion about earplugs, bought a pair today and tested them in the store parking lot by turning up the car radio as loud as it could go. They worked fine. The music from the light show shouldn't interfere with her writing one bit.

And he and April had been so nice, bringing her a tree.

And she had been—

Ungrateful.

But when she saw the little tree, all she could think about was Christmas morning alone. Christmas dinner alone. Maybe she should have accepted one of the offers to spend the holiday at a friend's.

But she wasn't interested in Christmas with just anyone. Her mind kept returning to the idea of Christmas with Kyle and April.

If only she could move past her fear, maybe invite them over for cocoa on Christmas afternoon. But what if they welcomed her into their lives, perhaps even invited her to eat Christmas dinner with them, simply because she was the lonely neighbor? What if once the holiday was over and she went back to her apartment, they moved on with their lives?

She'd be alone.

Hurting worse than she already was.

She couldn't take that chance.

But none of that excused her rudeness about the tree.

What she needed was a polite, careful apology, and another word or two of thanks for the tree. Once she unloaded her groceries and hauled in the twenty-five-pound bag of dog food, she would talk to them.

Then she would barricade herself, her groceries, and Jellybean in the main house.

Lanie rounded the last curve before the Mattoxes'.

And slammed on the brakes.

She'd seen the lights. And heard how loud the music was. And she'd known tonight was the first night of the light show.

But she'd never dreamed that there would be a line of cars backed up half a mile to see it. Now she understood the sign, "Please park only on this side."

At least they had.

Even so, the county road was narrow—too narrow for cars to park on one side and two other cars to pass. If someone came toward her from the other direction while she passed the parked cars, it would be a game of chicken.

But she needed to get to the main house. She was tired and cold, and she had mountains of groceries to put away.

Lanie edged forward, poked the front end of her car out to the left, and peered ahead. Nothing coming. She squared her shoulders and pulled forward.

But no one came from the other direction. She reached the driveway with no problem, then glanced right, ready to pull in.

And her face grew hot. Three cars blocked the way up to the main house.

Lanie laid on the horn.

No response.

Probably no one had even heard her over the chorus of "I Want a Hippopotamus for Christmas."

Lanie squeezed between two cars and parked on the snow beside the drive. She yanked her knit cap down harder on her head and climbed out. Snow slid in over the top of her left boot. With a snarl, she stomped up to an ancient Chevy Cavalier and rapped on the window.

A skinny woman wearing threadbare gloves rolled it down. Three young kids sat lined across the back in car seats. "I'm so sorry. Do you live here?" Her forehead wrinkled and her words tumbled out, nervous. "It was so crowded." She angled her head toward the cars parked along the road. "We always come the first night, and I wanted my kids to see the show before I had to take them to my mom's and go clock in, but I'll move my car."

Lanie's stomach bunched into a knot. Kyle was right. The light show was a big deal. "Oh, no." Lanie's voice came out high. "I just wanted to be sure you saw where I parked, kind of on the side there." She pointed.

The woman nodded. "I'll be very careful backing out," she said, her tone respectful.

"Thanks." Lanie felt even worse. Of course the woman would be careful. Everything about her said money was too tight not to be.

"It probably sounds silly," the woman said in a quiet voice, "but having this show, for free, way out here in the middle-of-nowhere in Abundance always seems like one more way he shows how much he loves us." She gestured to Lanie's necklace.

Lanie raised a hand to the cross. With all that had happened, she had a hard time trusting God. She kept seeing sign after sign that he didn't care. Part of her wanted to throw the necklace away. But she didn't. It seemed like if she did, things might get worse. So she wore it, a Christian good-luck charm that she didn't want to jinx.

Lanie gave a lame wave. "Merry Christmas."

"Merry Christmas to you. And God bless you and your family for doing this show." The woman waved, then raised her window, which went up in slow, erratic jerks.

Lanie walked back to her car, opened the trunk, and grabbed four plastic bags of groceries, two in each hand, to haul to the house. She had nothing to complain about. A warm place to stay, all this food . . .

With a thunk, she set the bags back in the trunk. Then she moved a box of graham crackers, a jar of peanut butter, and a package of clementines all to one bag. Before she let herself reconsider, Lanie knocked on the woman's car window again and held the bag out, pulling back the plastic to show the fruit. "Would your kids like these? As a snack while they watch the lights?"

For a second the woman looked at her, jaw muscles stiff, about to say no.

"Someone brought me a lovely Christmas gift today," Lanie said. "I feel like I ought to pass on the spirit."

The woman's face softened and she reached out to accept the bag. "Thank you. I'm keeping my neighbor's boy while she works a double shift." She tilted her head toward the toddler in the middle of the backseat. "He loves fruit."

Lanie smiled, then ducked away and headed toward her car, listening as the light-show music changed to the soft strains of "Away in a Manger."

Jellybean still had plenty of dry food in the main house. For now, she could bring in her perishable groceries and think about what to say to Kyle and April. Not some stiff excuse of an apology, but one that was heartfelt.

Chapter Four

The next morning, with all visiting vehicles gone, Lanie hiked to her car at the end of the driveway.

The air was warmer, and her boots crunched through the top layer of snow into the softer, squishy snow beneath. A male cardinal called from a low branch of a red cedar. As Lanie passed the tree, its scent reminded her of childhood, of Christmas at her grandparents'.

Farther toward the cottage, she passed the wooden frames and wires of the light show, all disarmed, a silent reminder of her need to apologize to Kyle and April. Lanie looked at a light in one of the cottage windows, but early Monday morning was not the time to drop by.

Best to concentrate on getting her car. She climbed in and put it in drive. Stepped on the gas and—

Spun her tires.

Lanie jerked the gearshift into park. Lovely, just lovely. She climbed out and stomped through the snow. From the back of the vehicle she could see the problem. The gravel driveway had been raised about a foot when it was built, probably to let rain run off. She had parked off the driveway, and she'd made things worse by grinding her tires down through the wet snow into mud.

Lanie swallowed and got in the car again. Then she tried to roll backward so she could get a running start, but the car didn't budge.

Worry built inside her. Once again she climbed out and stared at her rear tires, her arms crossed over her chest. Maybe the Mattoxes had sand in their garage that she could use to gain some traction. If not, twenty-five pounds of dog food was quite a load to haul through the snow to the main house. With a sigh, she trudged up the drive.

"Hi, Miss Lanie," April called from behind her.

Lanie turned and waved.

"Need a push?" Kyle strode toward her.

His wavy hair had a casual tousle, and his cheeks were freshly shaved. And his gray dress coat looked too conservative for a man running such an over-the-top Christmas display.

"Thanks, but you'd ruin your shoes," Lanie said.

Kyle stopped and tucked his pant legs into tall boots hidden beneath them. "Not to worry. As the new guy at the hospital, I have terrible parking. My good shoes are in here." He raised his messenger bag, then handed it to his daughter. "April, hold this and stand by the reindeer."

April took the bag and moved out of the way.

He made shooing motions toward Lanie, as if he needed to get this done and head to work.

Lanie climbed in the car and rolled down her window.

"Okay, give it gas gently," Kyle yelled from behind the car.

"What if I slide backward?"

"I'll move," he said, without a trace of concern. "I've done this before. I lived in Chicago."

Lanie started the engine and nudged the gas.

The car made a grinding noise but didn't move.

"A little more," Kyle shouted. In the rearview mirror she could see his jaw tight, his face red.

She gunned it.

And the car surged onto the driveway.

Success. She hit the brakes and slid it into park.

Near the reindeer, April cheered.

Kyle walked up beside the car.

Lanie leaned out her window. "Thank you."

"No problem."

"And thank you for the tree. I'm sorry I was grumpy yesterday," she said. "Please tell April I really like it." She settled back behind the wheel, ready to drive away.

But that apology sounded lame. She couldn't leave it at that. She looked back at him. "My sister and her family moved away right after Thanksgiving." Lanie's cheeks grew hot and she glanced at the steering wheel, then forced herself to go on. "And last February my mom died. This season is . . . hard."

Kyle's gloved hand covered her mitten, somehow warming her hand and her heart at the same time.

"I'm sorry." His voice was gentle.

She glanced up. Tiny lines fanned out from his brown eyes, as if he truly cared.

A look of uncertainty flashed across his face, then he stepped closer. "April and I are decorating cookies tonight. Her idea. Would you like to join us? You could bring Jellybean."

Lanie pulled her hand back. Exactly what she didn't want—a sympathy invitation. "I wouldn't want to intrude."

"You wouldn't be. We'd love to have you."

He sounded sincere. A bubbly feeling welled up in her heart, a feeling that only intensified when she looked at the kindness in his eyes, the firm line of his jaw, and his broad shoulders. It might be fun, but—

"Seven thirty. We'll be getting home from practice." He gave a sheepish shrug. "For the pageant."

He looked so dejected, like a little boy whose team had lost on the playground, that she almost laughed. "Couldn't talk her out of it, huh?"

"Nope." He lifted one eyebrow. "Will you join us tonight? I could use an ally, especially if you know how to use an oven."

For a second her mouth dropped open. "Surely you know how to—"

A teasing grin spread across his face. His eyes, though, invited her to laugh with him.

Lanie's chest filled with warmth. "I'll be there." The words slipped out as if some other, braver person had said them.

But she couldn't back out.

And deep inside, she didn't want to.

ෆ

Stupid. Stupid. Stupid.

One minute he was being a good neighbor, pushing Lanie's car out of the snow. The next minute he was inviting her over to make Christmas cookies.

Not the thing to do if a man wanted to keep his daughter from getting hurt.

And in less than five minutes, Lanie would be in his house, probably thinking he was interested in her. Maybe even seeing this as some kind of date.

Kyle parked his car by the cottage. At least practice had ended on time.

He unlocked the front door, steered April toward her bedroom to pack her backpack for childcare tomorrow, and started shoving dinner dishes in the dishwasher.

Now that he knew why Christmas was difficult for Lanie—especially since it had nothing to do with him—a date with her was not without its attractions. He'd never seen April take to someone so fast. And the way Lanie had looked at him when she accepted his invitation, with her blue eyes shining and a nervous smile, it made him feel—fine, he wasn't saying it out loud, but he could admit it to himself—it made him feel almost invincible.

But the woman was an art teacher. Flaky. Not someone you could depend on. Not someone you could trust.

No. He needed to make it perfectly clear—to Lanie and to April—that the tree and the cookies were friendly gestures, nothing more.

"My backpack's ready for tomorrow." April raced into the kitchen and pulled the cookie sheet out from the drawer under the stove. "It's so-ooo cool that you invited Miss Lanie."

Kyle held his hands palms up in a no-big-deal gesture. "Just being neighborly, like with Suzi's family."

"But Suzi's mom is a boring old writer, not an art teacher." April's voice took on a tone of reverence. "I bet Miss Lanie is amazing at decorating cookies."

"We'll see." Kyle could think of one artist who hadn't been big on baking. Hadn't been big on anything related to home and family. But he wasn't going to mention her. Especially not with April dancing around the living room in time to the light-show music like an elfin princess. No way he was making her sad.

The doorbell rang and April bolted toward the door.

"Remember," he shouted, "I have to make sure it's her before you open the door."

He lifted a magnet from the front of the fridge, removed a photo, and tucked it under a pile of bills on the island. By the time he got to the door, it was already open, Jellybean was thumping April with her tail, and Lanie was leaving her snowy boots on the doormat. She stepped inside, surrounded by a swirl of tiny snowflakes and that sweet coconut smell.

April launched herself at Lanie's legs. Lanie bent down to her level and hugged her. "We're going to have a fun evening, aren't we, cutie pie?"

"Daddy bought two packages of cookie dough and white frosting and sprinkles and four colors of frosting with the special tips you can draw with."

"I love those," Lanie said. The two of them giggled like co-conspirators.

"May I take your coat?" Kyle stepped closer to Lanie and placed a hand on the back of her coat collar.

She eased out of it and turned, her hair falling across his hand.

Under her coat she wore navy-blue leggings with small snowflakes on them and a navy dress-like thing with a giant, fuzzy white snowflake on the front. A tunic—he'd seen things like it when shopping for April.

Only not quite like it.

His pulse quickened.

He ignored it and hung up her coat. It too smelled faintly of coconut. He inhaled, then turned back around.

Tonight was neighborly.

Friendly.

Not a date.

But he still needed to make conversation. "So, uh, come on in. How's the thesis going?" Great. He sounded like he was the shy one, not April.

"Slow. I sent the first three chapters to my advisor today, but I'd worked on them before break. Once I have my master's, though, there's a school in St. Louis I want to apply to. They only hire teachers with advanced degrees. I have a friend who works there."

Kyle gave a nod of understanding and led the way into the kitchen. Moving to St. Louis made sense. But somehow it seemed like a bad idea.

"I have to tell you, April has high hopes for your decorating abilities," he said, more at ease with a project to focus on. He set out two logs of store-bought dough. "My artistic talent may be a little, um ... lacking."

April dug scissors out of a drawer and, standing right beside Lanie, attacked one of the logs, trying to remove the wrapper. "Daddy tried to draw a reindeer yesterday, but before I knew it was a reindeer"—her eyes sparkled—"I told him it was a really good picture of Jellybean."

Lanie hid her grin behind her hand, her eyes scrunched up in laughter.

"In my defense, I had not yet drawn the antlers," Kyle said, feigning indignation. "But still, it's good you're here. I might have trouble using the stove." He winked at her.

Lanie rolled her eyes. "I'm happy to be here," she said to April. "When I was little, I loved decorating cookies with my mom and dad. It felt so cozy. My nephews have never seemed interested. They're four and six." Her voice held that note that one woman uses to complain to another about men. "They think cookies are only for eating."

"When Daddy was little, he helped with the light show, just like me," April said.

Lanie looked at him. "Did you grow up around here?"

"No, but we visited every Christmas. A huge family event with tons of cousins. It was great. I think that's when I first got interested in electronics and computers." Kyle took a knife out of the drawer for slicing the dough.

Lanie looked at the knife with a frown.

Did she think he was some loser dad, planning to let April use it?

"Do you have any unflavored dental floss?" Lanie said.

"I'll get it," April said, and she rushed down the hall.

"What for?" he asked.

"You'll see. An art teacher learns to be very resourceful." Lanie gave a knowing look.

April returned with the floss. Lanie wrapped a strand of it around the log of dough once and pulled, creating a round slice instead of a perfectly good oval one like Kyle had made in the past.

April, mesmerized, took each round slice and placed it gently on the cookie sheet.

Kyle started a pot of decaf. Then he leaned back against the counter, listened to the light-show music, and stared at Lanie's hair. It had been so soft when he'd helped her with her coat. She and April didn't even notice he wasn't helping. They were too busy with the cookies.

Once they were baked, Kyle fixed April hot cocoa and poured two mugs of coffee. By the time they had sampled a few unfrosted cookies, April began to fade. She managed to decorate eight cookies before she yawned.

And then the music stopped. No wonder April was tired. It was nine, her bedtime over the school break. Kyle tapped her on the shoulder. "Why don't you decorate one more, brush your teeth, and I'll tuck you in."

April protested, but he reminded her that she needed to be well rested at practice for the pageant the next day. Ten minutes later he carried her to bed, her head nestled on his shoulder. He tucked her under the covers, toy elephant in her arms, and kissed her forehead. By the time he walked to the door of the room, she was asleep.

For a moment he stood in April's doorway like he did every night, gazing at the curve of her cheek in the night-light, grateful to have her in his life. Then he walked back into the hall.

And stopped short.

In the kitchen, Lanie leaned over the table, a frosting tube in each hand, focused on the cookies. She looked up, and the overhead light hit just right, intensifying the blue of her eyes.

He gulped. No way was he letting the invitation this morning lead to other problems.

With long, quick strides, he walked into the kitchen and pointed at the cookies. "These look great," he said. Polite and friendly, nothing more.

She added a red bow to a holly leaf she had drawn on a cookie, then stood up. "April is such a darling girl." She gave him an appreciative smile that went straight to his heart.

All right, so the woman was intelligent. Not an excuse for him to do something foolish. "Uh, thanks. I'm glad you could come over this evening." He grabbed his coffee mug.

"It was nice of you to invite me. I almost—" Lanie's voice grew more quiet and she scooted two cookies over, aligning them into a neat row. "I almost said no. I, uh, got really burned at a social event a few Christmases ago. Not literally, of course." She glanced toward the stove. "But, you know . . ."

"I'm divorced. I know." And he knew the exact social event she meant. He moved to the sink and ran some water over the cookie sheet. Somehow he felt better with the kitchen table between them.

Lanie looked at him like she wanted more explanation.

"My ex-wife just . . . just left. She was a painter, said she had to pursue her 'art.'" Bitterness crept into his tone and he scrubbed the cookie sheet. "April was still a baby. About a year ago, Tiffany married some guy who makes found object sculptures, piles of trash that he sells for five figures. And poor April. It's like she never mattered."

For a second, Lanie didn't respond.

Kyle's chest tightened. He should have kept his mouth shut. His past was none of her—

"The poor thing." Lanie brought a hand to her heart. "My dad divorced my mom when I was seven. Moved away, had a new family in Arizona." Her voice became low and wobbly. "Believe me, I understand that you want April to feel like she matters."

Then Lanie was beside him, her hand on his shoulder. "I'm so sorry."

Sympathy filled her eyes, like she really cared. Like she was different.

Kyle mumbled his thanks and put the cookie sheet on the drying rack, but he couldn't think what to say next.

The room seemed warmer. The air, thicker. His vocal chords, useless.

Lanie snagged a cookie from the table and held it toward him. "Want to try one, now that they're decorated?"

The silence would seem normal if he were eating.

He dried his hands on a towel and took a bite, trying to focus on the sweet cookie, the creamy frosting.

Lanie took a step back, as if she knew she'd come too close emotionally. And too close physically.

The distance didn't help.

Kyle's mouth grew dry, and all he could think about was Lanie.

His eyes locked on her, and he felt on the table for his coffee, found the mug, took a sip.

And stood at the edge of the ocean with the tide rushing out, the sand sinking away beneath him, moving him toward her whether he wanted to or not.

She looked up, and the sympathy in her eyes faded, changing into something warmer, inviting.

Kyle set down his coffee, closed the distance between them, and wrapped her in his arms.

She turned, aligning their bodies, and her blue eyes grew dark.

He drew her nearer and threaded his hands into her hair, letting it flow over his fingers. Soft. So soft.

Her lips parted.

Heat poured through his body and he lowered his mouth to hers.

He could taste frosting on her tongue. Could smell sugar cookies and a faint hint of coconut. Could hear a log shift in the fireplace, hear the flames crackle.

She moved closer until their bodies touched.

And everything dissolved into the background.

Everything except Lanie.

Everything except their kiss.

Slow and sincere and sweet.

At last, his control crumbling, he stepped back.

Her eyes fluttered open, her pupils wide.

His heart pounded against his chest and he brushed his fingertips across her cheek. "The cookies are . . . delicious."

"They are." Her voice held a note of wonder and she gave a slow nod. "Way better than I expected."

Chapter Five

Lanie ignored her phone buzzing on the dining room table the next morning.

She never should have mentioned the plans to make cookies when Megan texted yesterday. But her big sister was nothing if not persistent. If Lanie didn't answer, the texts and phone messages would pile up, as if Megan had a right to every tidbit of her life.

Lanie grabbed the phone and walked to the living room. On the rug in front of the fire, Jellybean raised her head, then went back to sleep.

"Well, how was it? Did you have fun?" Although Megan was past thirty, she only needed a mention of a man in Lanie's life to sound like she was back in high school.

"I did." Lanie kept her tone flat, like a frequent suspect in an interrogation room.

"Are you going to see him again?"

"I don't know." Lanie gazed out the front window toward the cottage. Drips of snow plunked off the trees.

"Do you want to? Does he want to?" Megan's words flew, fast and eager.

"Probably." Lanie gave a silent sigh. She knew what was coming.

"I just have a feeling this guy has real potential. Why don't you fix a big pot of soup and invite them over for supper?"

Trust Megan to jump on any chance to pair Lanie with a man. And to have advice at the ready.

Lanie slid a glance toward the kitchen. She could make soup and invite them over. They could eat at the round, wooden table, all cozy in the kitchen. And if Kyle happened to kiss her again . . .

But what if he did and the kiss didn't mean anything to him?

"Lanie? Are you there?" Megan's voice grew louder.

"What?"

"I said, if you'd like, I could e-mail you a bunch of soup recipes."

"Um, no. No soup." Lanie scrambled up off the couch. "I have to write this thesis. Bye." She clicked off before Megan could try to change her mind.

If Kyle wanted to see her again, he could ask. She wasn't rushing in and making herself all vulnerable. And she wasn't going to risk missing her deadline.

No way was she disappointing Mom. Lanie had promised her that she would graduate. Maybe even stretched the truth a bit near the end when Mom asked how it was going. If Lanie had been honest, had said there was no way to write a thesis while you watched a parent battle cancer, Mom would have been devastated. Truth was, it had been all Lanie could do to make lesson plans and get through her teaching days.

The half-truths she'd told her mom could only be made right if she actually finished her thesis and earned her degree, which meant she needed to quit dawdling.

Lanie moved her chair and laptop slightly so her back was directly toward the fire. She sent a quick e-mail to Kelly to let her know that Jellybean was fine, then checked for a response from her advisor.

Nothing.

No matter. Lanie dug out her notes for chapter 4 and started typing the first paragraph.

She worked steadily. At noon she carried a ham sandwich to the keyboard and slogged onward.

Finally, by three, chapter 4 was half done. She checked her e-mail once more and found a reply from her advisor.

Lanie,

I needed all of your chapters, not just the first three, yesterday.

As I said in my e-mail earlier this month, my plans changed and I am leaving the country this Saturday, Dec. 17. Although I allowed an extension when you faced personal issues, the university has a strict policy about the maximum time allowed for a master's program. If you want to complete your degree, I must forward your thesis, after you have made my corrections, to the Graduate Office before I leave.

Your first three chapters were strong. If the remaining chapters are complete and are also well written, I will try to help you finish on time.

Carol Anthwhite

Lanie's throat tightened. She reread the words on the screen, then searched through old e-mails. And found no notification of her advisor's holiday plans. Anywhere.

Her hands shaking, she pounded out an e-mail, biting back her anger and politely informing her advisor that she was asking the impossible, that Lanie had thought she was on the original time line, that she had two whole weeks to write the last three chapters.

Less than a minute after Lanie sent it, she received a reply—and a miserly extension. The last three chapters were due tomorrow evening at eight. Her advisor would return them Friday morning. All corrections were due Saturday morning at nine.

The tension in Lanie's throat spread until her whole body was rigid, and she struggled for a gulp of air. She wanted to scream, wanted to pound out horrible sounds from the baby grand, wanted to call her advisor and say she was giving up. But if she was going to graduate, she had two and a half more chapters to finish. By the end of the day tomorrow.

If she didn't finish, she'd be failing her mom.

For a long moment she sat there gripping the edge of the table, staring at the black letters of the message on the screen. Outside, in the bleak winter day, the snow dripped away, bit by bit, like the seconds of the time she had left.

Last night she'd wasted hours—hours—making cookies.

She was not giving up. She was not going to fail.

And she certainly was not making soup for Kyle and April.

She'd be lucky to have time to eat.

☙

A hoard of children poured out of the sanctuary into the church lobby, bouncing and shouting as though the choir director had passed out energy drinks instead of juice boxes halfway through practice.

In the sea of puffy coats, Kyle spotted April.

He waved at Becky Hamlin, the choir director, corralled his daughter, and led her out to the parking lot.

Finally. They both needed a quiet evening. One with no excitement. No Lanie.

Not that last night was her fault. He was the one who'd invited her over.

And the one who kissed her.

One misstep after another.

The woman was moving to St. Louis. From now on, no matter how understanding Lanie was—or how attractive—he was keeping his distance.

April climbed in the backseat. "Daddy, I need angel wings."

"No problem." He watched April fasten her seatbelt.

"Dress rehearsal's the day after tomorrow."

The day after tomorrow? Two days away? Kyle glanced back toward the church, where he could see the director standing inside the door. She had seemed like a nice, reasonable person. But two days' notice was not reasonable.

"My new friend, Missy, has wings you can see through, like the sleeves on my princess nightgown. Only white. And they sparkle. We should go to the store now."

Kyle pulled out of the church lot and headed home. "Sorry, sweetheart, we need to go home. You barely had time for a snack before practice. You need dinner."

"It will only take a minute. We just need a pattern and the sparkly material."

Kyle passed the road that led to the main shopping area. "April, I can't sew. I'll order you something online." Overnight shipping would be outrageous, but he'd pay it.

"But Miss Hamlin doesn't want parents ordering wings already made, doesn't want people to spend that much money."

Kyle squeezed the steering wheel with both hands. One of those teachers. The kind who assumed that every parent was artistic and had a closet of craft supplies at home. Sadly, he'd been down this road when April was in preschool. He might as well face the inevitable. "All right, we'll go to the store tomorrow."

"Tomorrow we need to make them." April's words came out faster, more agitated.

Kyle stared at the road ahead. He was hungry. And he could barely make a stick figure. There had to be a way out of this.

"Everyone else had their costumes today. Miss Hamlin said she sent you an e-mail about costumes when you signed me up."

Kyle tightened his grip on the steering wheel. There had been an e-mail. He hadn't opened it. Putting the word "costumes" in the subject line was like mailing someone an envelope marked "anthrax." And he had been totally crushed at work. Still, he should have read it. "Are you sure you're not hungry?"

"Not at all."

After fifteen minutes in the fabric and craft department, and what could only be termed an intervention by the grandmotherly woman working there, he learned that the pattern required sewing. With a machine. And something called interfacing.

"Do you think they have any leftover Halloween costumes? Maybe a fairy princess?" he asked the saleswoman. Could she tell from his voice that he'd be willing to go in the stockroom and climb on the high shelves to look?

She shook her head, her lips drawn in.

April's face was pale, her eyes getting that almost-teary look. He knew this trip was a bad idea, especially after letting her stay up late last night.

"How about we buy poster board, cut out wings, and decorate them with glitter?" Kyle said. April loved glitter. "We could even look for a silver glitter pen—maybe as part of a ten-pack of different colors."

A woman shopper walked by, completely ignoring the screaming toddler standing in her cart, and rolled her eyes. Kyle glared at her. So technically buying a ten-pack of glitter pens would be a bribe, but she wasn't in the running for parent of the year either, letting her kid stand in the cart.

"This isn't preschool," April said, sounding desperate to make him understand. "The kids' costumes are real."

Kyle took her hand and led her away from the fabric department. "If you need it Thursday, that's the best I can do, sweetheart. Daddy's not any good with crafts."

She gave a brave smile. "I know. You're better with computers. But you're still the best dad ever." Her voice held a faint tremor, as if it took everything she had to hold back her tears.

A lump grew in Kyle's throat and he pulled her close. An inability to craft angel wings should not make him feel like he was due a visit from a state social worker.

But it did.

And it meant the perfect Christmas for April was never going to happen.

Then she stepped back and looked up at him, tears gone. "Let's call Miss Lanie. I bet she knows how to make wings."

"I'm sure she's busy, working on her thesis," Kyle said, although the idea of dumping the project on Lanie sounded brilliant. She probably enjoyed crafts.

"Could we call her and ask?" April unhooked Kyle's cell phone from his belt holster and held it toward him. "She might say yes."

Kyle took the phone and ran his thumb back and forth across the screen. Hadn't he vowed twenty minutes ago that he didn't need any more time with Lanie Phillips?

"Please?" April drew the word out like Lanie was their last hope.

Kyle didn't own a sewing machine. Didn't know how to use one. Didn't have a clue what interfacing was. And sure didn't want to disappoint April.

He dialed Aunt Kelly and Uncle Rich's number.

"Kyle, hi." Lanie sounded rushed.

"Hi, I hate to bug you, but April needs angel wings by Thursday. For the pageant."

Lanie didn't reply.

"Uh, I wasn't asking you to make them or anything," Kyle added, talking fast. "I just wondered if you know a way to make wings that look good but that doesn't involve sewing."

"There is a way but"—her voice grew tight—"I'm really behind on my thesis."

"Please. I'm desperate."

There was a long pause. Kyle pressed the phone closer against his ear, as if that might make her talk. If her method was easier than sewing, how hard could it be to explain?

"Okay." She spoke quickly, like she begrudged him every word. "Buy a sheet of poster board and a couple packs of big coffee filters, like for a twelve-cup coffee maker. Does she need a halo too?" Lanie's tone implied that a halo might be the ultimate imposition.

Kyle didn't care. "Halo?" he mouthed to April.

She nodded, her eyes wide.

"Yes," he said into the phone.

"So, gold pipe cleaners. And about three yards of white ribbon and some school glue. Buy the stuff and bring it over tomorrow night. I'll show you what to do." Lanie hung up.

Kyle ran back through the list, counting each item on his fingers. Five things.

He'd buy them. But coffee filters didn't sound like the makings of very good wings.

And Lanie didn't sound like she even cared. She sounded like she didn't have time for him. Or April. A lot like Tiffany.

Keeping his distance would not be a problem.

Chapter Six

The next evening, Kyle knocked on the door of the main house. Six fifteen. He had exactly one hour and fifteen minutes before he had to pick up April from practice, and he needed to learn how to make those wings.

If Lanie would hurry up, he might even have time to work on them some before he had to drive back to town.

"What?" Lanie opened the door. She sounded—and looked—off-balance, like he'd woken her up. Tufts of hair stuck out of her ponytail on both sides of her head.

Kyle held up two plastic shopping bags. "The wings?"

"I'm really busy. Can we do it tomorrow evening?" Her face was drawn, and she edged the door shut.

"Tomorrow evening April has to wear them."

He moved closer to the door. He was not leaving, not until she helped him. After that she could be as busy as she liked. He'd be more than happy to leave her alone. Because she was just like Tiffany. She didn't see April as a priority.

"Okay, okay, if we can do this really fast." Lanie sounded exasperated, but she let him inside, then quickly led him into the kitchen.

"Fast is good." Kyle followed along.

In the living room, the fire was out, and ashes had been spilled on the carpet in front of the hearth. The dining room table—and the floor around it—were scattered with wadded balls of printer paper. Although Jellybean's food and water bowls were full, an empty potato chip bag and three dirty mugs were piled by the kitchen sink. And Lanie didn't even smell of coconut.

She grabbed a small notebook and a pen. "First, you cut out wings from the poster board. You want to have a little tab to connect them, like this." In a matter of seconds, she sketched two wings on the pad.

Kyle nodded once. He could handle that.

"Then you start folding the coffee filters. Bunch up several at once into kind of a tent, like you're pomping." Lanie glanced at the clock on the stove and her jaw tensed.

"Pomping?" Kyle said.

"Like for a parade float." Lanie looked at him as if the word was common knowledge.

"I never made a parade float."

She took the coffee filter package from his hand, ripped it open, and pulled out the top three.

Outside, the light-show music changed, shifting into "All I Want for Christmas Is My Two Front Teeth." Not Kyle's personal favorite, and apparently not Lanie's either, from the way she flinched at the first notes. Still, it was a crowd pleaser, according to Uncle Rich.

Lanie folded the coffee filters into a little wedge. "Like this."

Kyle wasn't the most observant guy, but her hand was shaking. Something was bothering her—besides the music. Did he want to ask?

Not really.

Lanie threw the coffee filters on the counter. "I'm sorry. I can't do this now. But I'll make the wings for you tomorrow morning. Measure the width of April's shoulders. I'll give you my number so you can text it to me."

No doubt Lanie would do a better job than he would, so her offer ought to make him happy. It didn't.

Because she looked and sounded so . . . fragile. Like by simply stopping by he was pushing her over the edge.

"Hey." He spoke in a hushed tone, took a step toward her, and rested the fingers of one hand on her shoulder. "What's going on?"

"I have to e-mail the last three chapters of my thesis to my advisor by eight tonight. Or I'm basically kicked out of the program." The tendons in her throat tightened, and with each word her voice grew higher, more panicked. "I only found out yesterday. Really, I will make the wings in the morning. After I sleep."

Without thinking, he rubbed his fingers in small circles on her shoulder, the same way he soothed April. Kicked out was serious. More serious than a costume for a pageant that wasn't for four days.

Her shoulder muscles stayed bunched under his fingers, knotted and unyielding.

"Worry about the wings later." He looked at the sink again. Three cups. Not a single plate. "What have you eaten today?"

"A can of tomato soup." She wrapped her arms over each other. "And most of—" She too looked at the counter. "All of a bag of chips."

Potato chips wouldn't cut it, especially if she'd been up all night. Kyle kept his hand on Lanie's shoulder and steered her toward the dining room table, like he did when it was time for April to practice reading. "You sit. And write. I'll restart the fire and bring you dinner."

She looked up at him, her face a bit less tense. "That would be great. I promise I'll make the wings tomorrow. You know—" Her voice caught. "You know I adore April."

"I know." He swallowed hard and stepped back. He owed her some explanation, given how pushy he'd been. "I get a little freaked out if I think I'm going to fail her."

"I understand." Her words were gentle, like a balm.

Kyle nodded. She did understand. She wouldn't hurt April. She wasn't like Tiffany.

She was a good person.

A scratchy knot rose in his throat.

He should be a good person as well. He should tell her the truth about her wedding.

But he couldn't do it. Not now. Not when she was already overwhelmed.

He looked away. "Uh, thank you. For now, though, we need to take the deadlines in order. First, your thesis."

She turned to her laptop—her plugged-in laptop. Should he say something? No, he would sound like some know-it-all.

He kept his mouth shut for three seconds, all he could manage, then spoke. "You shouldn't use your laptop plugged in all the time. On a lot of machines, it can be bad for the battery."

Lanie shook her head. "Too late. The battery died a month ago. I have to keep it plugged in."

"You really should replace—"

"I'd have to send it off. No time."

No, he guessed not. Not when she had to finish her thesis. But he could replace the battery, no problem. If he ordered one today, with two-day shipping...

Lanie reached for a pair of earplugs by her laptop.

"Do those really work?" he said.

"Actually, they do."

"Good." He exhaled. "I'll fix the fire, then let myself back in with your dinner." And he'd check the specs on her laptop so he could look online for a battery.

"Thank you." Lanie sounded stronger and a bit of life returned to her eyes. "I think I can finish those chapters if I give it one more push."

"You can," Kyle said, trying to sound encouraging.

She raised her chin, then picked up the earplugs and turned to the computer.

Kyle went out to the side of the house and gathered an armload of wood.

At the end of the drive, the light show blared.

Tonight, due to unforeseen circumstances, the music would be turned down.

It wasn't much, but it might help.

They were a team.

☙

As soon as Kyle's car pulled in the next evening, Lanie bundled up and walked down to the cottage. She knocked on the back door and held the angel wings high so April could see them through the window.

The little girl squealed and opened the door.

Last night, with only three minutes to spare, Lanie had shipped the chapters. Then she had crashed.

But bright and early this morning, she had been up, ready for the day. First she'd checked on Jellybean, then she'd looked for a reply from her advisor. Nothing yet.

Glad for a reprieve from thinking about her thesis, she'd started making the wings. Kyle had been so kind last night, building a fire, bringing her a big plate of spaghetti and meat sauce, even including two cookies for a treat "when she finished her chapters." Each coffee filter that Lanie folded to form a feather on the wings was a thank you to Kyle and a way to show April how much she mattered.

Now April carried the wings to the breakfast bar and shoved a pile of papers aside. She set the pair of wings down as carefully as if it were a baby bird, then gently touched the bottom edge.

In a flash she spun and launched herself at Lanie. "They're beau-tee-ful." She squeezed her arms around Lanie's waist as tight as a pair of size A pantyhose.

Her heart light, Lanie wrapped her arms around the girl.

April stepped back and ran her fingertips over the edge of the wings again. "Even prettier than Missy's. Thank you," she said in awe.

Lanie drew in a deep breath, trying to fill her chest with the love that surrounded her.

"Hey, Lanie," Kyle shouted from down the hall over the noise of the dryer. "I got a call from Aunt Kelly. My cousin Jill is better. Going home tomorrow."

"That's great."

"I'm just throwing in a second load of laundry before dinner. We're having grilled cheese, if you want some."

What looked like split-pea soup warmed in a pan on the stove, and grilled cheese sandwiches sat on a chopping board, filling the room with the aroma of melted butter. On the table, two places were set, and a bowl held oranges cut into smiles. And she was invited. Add another plate and she'd be part of the family.

Emotion welled up inside Lanie and she blinked back tears.

She looked down and spotted a new drawing by April on the counter. Another picture of Jellybean, but this time only the dog's head. Lanie lifted the paper up, about to comment on it, and stopped.

Underneath was a photo that... didn't make sense. Kyle and a bunch of guys, including a familiar face.

"April?" Lanie tapped the photo. "Who's this with your dad?"

"I don't know his name. Some old roommate."

An icy feeling grew at the base of Lanie's scalp, then raced down her spine and into her arms.

The man in the picture was her former fiancé, the fiancé who said he'd been convinced by his roommate that marrying her was a bad idea.

"Those look incredible." Kyle walked in and reached one hand toward the wings.

Lanie raised her head and stared at him, searching for the truth in his eyes. She didn't want to ask, but she had to know. "We need to talk. Outside. Now." She tried to keep her voice calm but, even to her, it sounded unsteady.

"All ri-ight." Kyle fixed a plate and set it on the kitchen table. "You eat dinner, April."

"But—" April started.

Kyle gestured toward the food.

Lanie's hands grew icy even before she walked out the back door into the damp, chilly air and the sloshy snow.

Kyle stepped outside behind her, closed the door, and moved several feet away from the house. "What's wrong?" He gave a quick, things-can't-be-that-bad smile. "Those wings are a work of art."

"I don't care about the wings," she said, moving back several inches. "Tell me how you know Derek."

The smile melted off Kyle's face. Understanding—then guilt—flashed across his eyes.

Which meant he'd known—all along—who she was. And meant that—as unlikely as it seemed, as much as she didn't want to believe it—he was *that* Kyle. God must have a twisted sense of humor to let this man come into her life.

"We were roommates our last year in college." His voice sounded hollow and his lips became a thin line.

Lanie's heart beat faster and faster, and her breath came hard and heavy. Heat built in her chest and poured through her, a boiling, bitter bile.

This man—the one she'd daydreamed over, the one she'd thought so kind last night, the one who'd kissed her like she was precious, like she was worth loving—was the very man who had shattered her past.

"I wanted to tell you, but it was never the right time." His words came out hurried, desperate.

"I think you had *plenty* of right times." Her pulse pounded in her temples. "But you"—she jabbed him in the chest—"you never said a thing." She punctuated each word with another thrust of her finger.

"Lanie, I—"

"You acted like you had no idea who I was. What a lie. And here I was thinking..." She trailed off and her hands fell, trembling at her sides. Then, her body shaking with adrenaline, she drew in a ragged breath and jammed her hands on her hips. "I cannot believe you ruined my life. Twice."

She spun on the heel of her boot and ran toward the main house, each step flinging mud and snow behind her.

She could hear Kyle scrambling to catch up. "Wait. Stop." His words pierced the air, echoing in the cold.

She turned back to face him. "No!" she screamed, holding up a hand to ward him off. "You stop. Stop following me."

Rage and pain piled inside her, choking her. Once again, she'd trusted. Once again, she'd been betrayed. Once again, Christmas meant heartache. "Leave me alone."

Chapter Seven

Lanie hunched over on the living room couch, a pillow clenched against her stomach, a tissue box at her side. Heat poured off her face and chest, and she dug into the box for another tissue.

Jellybean padded up beside her, nudged her head in, and laid it on Lanie's thigh.

A tear landed on Jellybean's head. Lanie smeared it into the soft fur, then blew her nose and rubbed her hands across her face. Her eyes stung and her sinuses had swollen shut.

She shoved the tissue in her pocket and ran her fingers over Jellybean's ears.

Her phone dinged with a text. As if she were expecting a death threat, she cautiously pulled the phone from her other pocket.

Let me explain. Please.

She clicked the window shut and set the phone down. But the message was still there, where she'd see it again. She reopened her messages, tapped Kyle's, and hit "Delete."

Better.

Night fell and she stared into the fire.

Kyle had known who she was all along. He might have even called Derek and shared a good laugh—at naïve, gullible Lanie.

Outside the window, the frames of the giant, light-up snowflakes came to life, and the light-show music blared. The minute Kyle was such a jerk about that music, she should have known to stay away from him.

Lanie let out a moan and went to the kitchen. Deep in a cabinet she found some old Halloween-size Butterfingers. She yanked the bag against her chest, retreated to the couch, and ripped open the package.

Should she call Megan? No. She turned the phone off. The situation was too horrible to talk about. She bit into the first Butterfinger. Not stale at all. All she wanted to do was lie on the couch and cry, eat the Butterfingers, then move on to her last bag of potato chips. The ache in her chest hurt so much that if she focused on it, the pain could suck her in, like the goo in the La

Brea Tar Pits trapped those poor creatures she'd seen on a TV special, the ones who became fossils.

Lanie unwrapped a second Butterfinger and chomped down on it. Halfway through the third, she stopped.

She wasn't about to be some prehistoric ground sloth, trapped forever in despair. Somehow, she would move forward. She grabbed the wrappers and took the candy bag back to the kitchen. No more. And no potato chips.

Time for some changes.

First, she had to think about April. How a creep like Kyle ended up with a darling girl like her defied all logic. The child must take after her mother. Kyle said his ex-wife had left to pursue her art. Most likely she'd left to get away from Kyle.

Anyway, Lanie was not about to miss April's pageant. She could slip in the back of the church, give the girl a big thumbs-up at the end, then leave.

Lanie shoved the candy back in the cabinet, far in the corner where she wouldn't see it, and squared her shoulders. Then she went to the computer and opened her e-mail.

Her advisor had sent a quick message, a promise to e-mail the final corrections first thing tomorrow morning.

Lanie sat up taller, her jaw set. Tomorrow she would make those corrections and polish her thesis until it gleamed. As soon as she had her degree, she'd apply for that job in St. Louis. If that didn't work, she'd check other places. One way or another, she was moving out of Abundance—as far away as possible from Kyle Mattox.

Away from his lies.

But what about the lies she told herself?

Her chest tight, she unhooked her cross necklace, let it flow through the fingers of one hand and pool in her other palm. For a long moment, she squeezed her fist around it. Some cheap piece of jewelry wasn't going to protect her, and it wasn't going to make any difference to God. Because God didn't care. Not about her.

Her eyes grew hot. She squeezed them shut and drew in a deep, full breath, as if the air itself might soothe the ache inside her.

It didn't. But at least she wasn't crying anymore. And she wasn't believing any more lies.

She stood, walked to the bathroom trash can, and let the necklace drop.

☙

"You said that after practice you'd explain." April clicked her seatbelt and looked up at Kyle. "Why were you and Miss Lanie yelling?"

He'd had more than an hour, known the question was coming, and he still didn't have an answer.

The thing he wanted most—a perfect Christmas for April—and he'd destroyed it. He'd known all along that April might get hurt.

And he'd let himself be drawn in by Lanie anyway.

Drawn into caramel-blond hair and huge blue eyes. Drawn into the fuzzy comfort that wrapped around his heart, warming the cold, dark corners whenever he saw her. Drawn into disaster.

"Was it the picture of you and that guy? Or"—April's voice grew tense, as if she was afraid to go on—"or was it me?"

"April." Kyle turned off the engine and spun to face her. "It was not your fault in any way. Miss Lanie adores you. I was the one who made her mad."

April's brows pulled together, the normal sparkle gone from her eyes.

Anxiety and self-accusation hardened into a lump in Kyle's stomach. "I'm sure Miss Lanie will still want to see you, though, especially when you have pictures to show her."

"You're sure?" April's faint words were edged with doubt.

He nodded, trying to hide his worry. If Lanie ignored April completely . . .

If only she'd never come into their lives. If only he'd waited until January to move.

April looked down at her wings, cuddled on her lap. "She won't," she said, all emotion gone from her voice. "She'll never spend time with me again."

○₃

The next night, close to seven, Lanie sat in a straight-back chair at the dining room table, shifting her weight. Her back ached from nine straight hours working on her laptop, but she was going to finish.

Outside in the darkness, the wind howled, sometimes loud enough to block out the noise from Kyle's beloved light show.

She stood, stretched, and added another log to the fire. A few feet from the hearth, Jellybean slept, her big tummy exposed, her chest rising and falling gently.

Lanie sat down again, tried to find a comfortable position, and failed.

It had been a marathon day for changes, but she'd stuck with it. Her advisor had suggested a massive rearrangement of the document, but now that Lanie had done it, it made sense. An hour ago, seeing the whole thesis in a new light, she'd added more analysis like her advisor wanted, two whole new pages in chapter 5, pages that seemed downright insightful, at least to her.

But her back and her right shoulder were killing her. No matter. She was so close.

Lanie scrolled through the pages, checking for misspelled words.

She found two typos, underlined in red, and fixed them.

A quivery excitement built in her chest, and she pressed her back against the chair, eyes fixed on the screen.

With a bit more polishing, she'd practically have her master's degree. Nothing but paperwork and a meeting with her committee, which her advisor promised Lanie would ace.

"Almost done," she whispered. "And more than twelve hours early."

ଔ

Man, it was a long way down.

Kyle never should have looked. He tightened his grip on the ladder that he'd propped against the big oak.

The wind lashed against him, cut right through his jeans, and screamed so loudly he almost couldn't hear the music from the light show.

He raised his chin and climbed up another step.

Some people might say hanging a decoration in a tree in the dark was a bad idea. But it wasn't just any decoration. It was an angel, and since April was an angel in the pageant, adding it to the light show was perfect.

Well, maybe not perfect, what with the wind whipping down out of the Arctic, but it was the only idea Kyle had to keep the fallout with Lanie from ruining his daughter's holiday. April could have her very own angel.

That ought to make her Christmas happier.

Right?

At least it was a start.

And the dark wasn't a problem. The light show was plenty bright. Plus, he'd taped a small flashlight to his antler cap, like a makeshift miner's helmet. He could see just fine.

He had thought the whole thing through. The base of the ladder was wedged into six inches of snow, the top nested in a V between two branches. He had attached the angel to the back of his jacket so he could use both hands to climb. And he had plugged in the angel's extension cord and brought a remote so he could test her on the same trip.

Logic and planning. Kyle gave a self-satisfied nod.

He took another step higher and the cord pulled on his jacket. The tug was unsettling, but he'd cope.

His gaze drifted to the main house. A grown woman should not throw a temper tantrum. He twisted his lips. Fine. So Lanie had a right to be angry, so he should have told her about Derek earlier. But he'd been waiting for the right moment. When did she want him to bring it up? When she had those chapters to finish and no sleep? Like that would have gone over well.

Kyle looked up, gauging how far he had to go. The higher he went, the darker it seemed, like he was climbing down into a hole, not up a tree.

As if soundtracked for his project, "Angels We Have Heard on High," floated up from the outdoor speakers.

Stupid song. The Gospel of Luke didn't specify where the angels were—Kyle had checked last night to be sure—but the song said "heard on high."

Not on the ground.

If God ever issued the Gospel of Luke, Version 2.0, Kyle might say a prayer or two to ask that it be specific. The angels probably sang over near the manger. On the ground. Out of the wind.

He went up one more rung and stopped. Good thing he didn't need to go higher. He'd almost reached the top.

He glanced down again, and fear pinched his spine.

Time to get this taken care of and get back on the ground. Kyle let go of the ladder with one hand and, reaching over his shoulder, removed the angel from a Velcro strap on the back of his jacket. Then he reached above his head and hung her by her halo on a fingerlike piece of branch, all that remained from a broken limb.

There, part one of the plan was complete.

For a second he looked at the branch and tried to convince himself it would hold the angel, even in the wind.

Not a chance. Time for part two.

His heart pounding, he leaned in toward the tree and let go of the ladder with both hands. Adrenaline pulsed through his veins, and his fingers shook as he started a nail to keep the angel in place.

Once the nail held, he grabbed the ladder with his left hand and used the hammer in his right hand to pound the nail home.

The angel secure, Kyle dropped the hammer to the ground.

Now, part three, testing.

He unzipped his jacket a few inches and pulled out the remote. With one gloved finger, he pressed "ON."

The angel stayed dark.

"Really, couldn't you just light up?"

He squinted through the night and tilted his head to shine the flashlight on the connector at the base of the angel's skirt.

It looked right, but . . .

Kyle bit into the tip of his glove, pulled it off, and held it between his teeth. With his bare hand, he squeezed the two parts of the connection closer together until they clicked into place.

The angel lit up—silver wings, white skirt, golden hair.

"Finally." Kyle put his bare hand on the icy ladder and gave the angel a victorious glare. All done.

Then he tried to put his fingers back in the glove he held in his teeth. But it was hopeless unless he used his other hand.

No way.

He was not taking both hands off the ladder. Not again. He opened his mouth and let the glove drop. He could find it in a few minutes.

From here, it should be easy. All he had to do was climb down the ladder and pick up his girl after practice.

He stretched one foot down.

Found the step.

Not a problem.

The light-show music shifted to a soft, gentle version of "Silent Night." Kyle inhaled deeply, savoring the scent of the nearby cedar trees. Christmas would work out. He and April would have a peaceful, happy holiday.

And then a horn blared.

Kyle spun and caught a glimpse of a big pickup barreling down the county road.

And realized he was airborne.

He was headed out one way, the ladder the other.

His heart pounded and his arms flailed like a kid who can't swim.

A branch flew by, then another, too fast to grab.

Then there was nothing to grab.

ଔ

The thesis was done.

And done well.

Pride welled inside Lanie's chest. She stretched her shoulders, sank back in the dining room chair, and slid her cursor toward the image of the disk to save the file.

Then, over the noise of the light show, there was a thump outside, as if a giant mass of snow had slid off the roof.

And the house went dark.

Including her laptop.

Her heart rate sped, ratcheting up notch by notch, one alarm bell after another sounding in her brain, and a lump like a golf ball formed in her throat.

"Oh, no." Her voice came out strangled.

For a few seconds, she tried to tell herself she'd hit "Save," tried to hold back the panic.

But she wasn't sure. Didn't really remember saving her work. Not since—

Since before she stopped to get more hot tea.

Before her insightful pages.

How long had that been? An hour? Two? She'd been so wrapped up in her brilliant ideas that she hadn't taken time to save. Just like she hadn't taken time to get her battery replaced.

Blood rushed through her veins and her breath grew shallow.

How much had she lost?

Chapter Eight

Kyle was in a pile of snow.

A pile of snow and a pile of pain.

But he couldn't get a full breath of air, couldn't understand what had happened. The ladder was not propped against the oak tree. And he was not Super Dad, climbing down steady and sure.

He was here, on his back, in the snowbank by the driveway to the big house. And he hurt.

Everywhere.

Tentatively he flexed his fingers, then raised his arms—one, then the other.

Painful, but bearable.

Then he moved his legs.

"Aaaagggghhh!" The cry exploded from him and his heart thundered. Adrenaline poured into his veins.

Icy sweat drenched him. He twisted his upper body to one side, a hand against his mouth, and fought down nausea.

The pain was white-hot and biting, like nothing he'd ever known.

He tried to breathe normally, tried to think.

There had been that idiot, racing down the road, blasting his horn, and Kyle had turned and—

He ground his teeth together. He knew all too well who the real idiot was.

And he knew his leg was broken.

With his right hand, nearly frozen without a glove, he grabbed for his belt holster.

No phone.

Maybe it had fallen off when he landed. He clawed an arm across the ground near his right side. Then his left. Another hit of adrenaline gushed into his system and he yanked the antler cap off. Without moving his leg a millimeter, he raised himself on his elbows and trained the flashlight attached to his cap on the snow around him.

No phone.

It must have been knocked off by a branch.

Which meant he couldn't call 911. Couldn't call the church. Couldn't tell anyone he wouldn't be there to pick up April after practice.

He lowered himself back to the ground. Then a worse thought slammed into his brain and his chest tightened. Even after his leg was in a cast, he wouldn't be able to drive. He'd broken his right leg.

He wouldn't be able to take April to practice or her performance. Wouldn't be able to drive to the store or pick up the last gifts he'd planned or fix dinner or do laundry. Christmas morning would be the two of them, eating cold hot dogs, sitting in the living room in dirty clothes, with him probably not even showered.

The perfect Christmas was a perfect catastrophe.

"Help! Hellllllllp!" he yelled as loudly as he could.

It was useless.

Day eight of "The Twelve Days of Christmas" boomed out from the speakers. No way anyone could hear him over those blasted maids a-milking.

And no way he could wait until the music ended or until someone came looking for him. April needed him.

And frankly, he needed painkillers.

He would have to move to where he could get someone's attention. The people in the cars along the road, enjoying the light show, were too far away. Even if he made it to his cottage, he didn't have a landline. He'd have to get to Lanie.

Kyle tugged his knit cap back on, shifted his body, and looked at the main house. He didn't remember her leaving, but all the lights were out.

Every single one.

He swung his head around and peered through the night at where the ladder had fallen, over near where—

Where the power line to the main house had dipped, ever since the last storm.

Unbelievable. He'd taken out her electricity.

But in the living room window, a light flickered. A candle or possibly a flashlight. Either way, it was proof Lanie was there.

Trying to keep his right leg immobile, he rolled to his left side, then onto his stomach. Pain filled every cell of his body, and a huge wave of nausea hit. He nearly threw up. For a few minutes he lay facedown on the snow, gasping for air, listening to the wind pick up.

If he didn't move, the leg throbbed. If he jostled it, his whole body burned with a spasm of agony.

But he was not going to fail April.

Propped up on his forearms, he slid his bare hand into his jacket sleeve and crawled army-style, letting both legs slide over the top of the snow with as few bumps as possible.

He was not leaving his daughter abandoned at the church. And he was not waiting here in the snow to freeze to death.

○₃

Lanie trained the flashlight on the living room floor, walked to the window, and peered out.

The light show had power. Kyle's cottage had power. Even the farmhouse across the road had power. The only place without power seemed to be the main house.

So not fair. And it didn't make sense. Unless Kyle had done something on purpose.

No. Even Kyle wouldn't leave her, wouldn't leave Jellybean, without heat. His aunt would kill him. And surely even he wouldn't be so horrid as to make her lose work on her thesis.

The muscles in Lanie's neck and shoulders stiffened, as if rebar had been inserted in them. What if she hadn't saved her file? Could she redo the corrections she'd lost, re-create those new pages?

Lanie closed her eyes and forced herself to take a slow breath. She could set up her laptop at her apartment. Maybe she'd even see that she had saved the file without thinking. She wanted to believe that. Wanted it bad.

Her landlord wouldn't be happy about Jellybean being there, but even he would understand that this was an emergency.

Before she could leave, though, she had to haul everything down that funny stairwell, into the garage that had been stuck on the back of the house.

With light from three candles she placed along the floor, Lanie began loading. First Jellybean's whelping box, towels, and dog food. Then easy stuff like her purse. Next her printer and laptop. At the weird corner on the stairs, her pulse quickened, and she lowered each foot with caution. There was no way to recover if she dropped her laptop.

At last she went back inside, grabbed the flashlight, and blew out the candles. "C'mon, Jellybean. We have to go across town."

The big dog followed her to the garage, not flustered a bit by the loss of electricity. If Lanie didn't know better, she'd swear Jellybean knew the word "town" and liked riding in the car. She opened the front passenger door, then hesitated. Hopping into the car might be too much for Jellybean. When Megan was nine months pregnant, Lanie didn't remember her doing anything more athletic than lifting a package of Oreo cookies.

But Jellybean hauled herself up easily.

"Good girl." Lanie tucked a blanket over her. "I know you like to be warm, and my car heater is slow."

She shut the car door and her nerves tightened. She'd been able to focus on loading, task by task. But now it was time to head across town. Time to find out how bad things really were.

Lanie released the emergency cord for the garage door and heaved the door open manually. Then, both hands clenched on the steering wheel, she backed out.

☙

Gasping for air, Kyle stopped and looked over his shoulder.

He'd gone ten feet. Ten measly feet. One hundred and twenty inches of torment.

He peered at the main house to see how much farther he had to go, how much more he had to endure.

And wished he'd never checked.

The wind gave a mighty blast and he let out a low moan. If only it wasn't so cold. Kyle wiggled the fingers of his right hand. They still had some feeling, but they were mostly numb. Keeping his hand in his sleeve was impossible. With his other hand, he pulled off his cap and wrapped it around his fingers. Maybe it would help.

He was not giving up. Kyle pulled himself forward another few inches. His chest burned with exertion and sweat dripped off his forehead into the snow. He squeezed his eyes shut and begged a silent prayer. "Help me, God."

He waited, but nothing changed.

Nothing.

The back of his throat tightened. No one to depend on but himself.

Kyle opened his eyes and looked at the main house.

The light was gone.

Lanie might still be tired from staying up all night the other day. With the electricity out, she might have gone upstairs to go to bed. And if she was asleep when he reached the house, she might not hear him knock.

He had to move faster.

Kyle raised himself on his hands and his good knee and tried to crawl. He lurched forward and jolted his bad leg. Pain burned through him, sending spasms through his whole body. The torment seemed alive, roaring in his ears.

No.

That roar wasn't the pain.

It was the engine of Lanie's car as she headed down the driveway.

Kyle forced himself up on his good knee. Then he wobbled and the bad leg hit the ground. The pain struck him like 240 volts of electricity. He struggled to breathe. His body reeled and blood pounded in his ears.

"Stop." He tried to yell but his voice creaked out, hoarse and faint.

Lanie kept driving.

ɞ

Icy air blew out the heat vents of Lanie's car. She turned the fan down and stepped on the gas, eager to reach her apartment and learn the truth about her thesis.

Outside, "Blue Christmas" poured from the loudspeakers, and to Lanie's right, toward Kyle's cottage, a trio of Christmas trees blinked. She drove past, then realized that in the snow in front of the three trees, she had seen something red. With . . . antlers.

She stopped the car and turned her head around.

That had to be Kyle. Whenever he worked on the light show, he wore a red ski jacket. But what was he doing on the ground? Was he hurt?

She rewrapped her scarf and climbed out, shutting the car door as quickly as possible to keep Jellybean warm.

"Blue Christmas" ended. The trio of trees went dark, making it harder to see.

"Lanie." He shouted and waved one arm at her.

"Kyle?" She ran toward him and stumbled in the snow, then steadied herself and moved closer.

"Call 911." His voice was gravelly. "My leg is broken."

"What happened?"

"Does it matter?" His tone held anger. And pain.

The lighting from the show changed again and she could see him more clearly. His face was drawn. One hand was bare—waxy and very pale. She scanned the area, looking for his glove.

She couldn't see a glove anywhere. But she did see a trail, where he'd been trying to crawl.

Her heart clenched and she raised a hand to her mouth. "I'll call." She ran back to the car for her phone and dialed.

"911 operator. What's your location?"

Lanie gave the address. "Halfway up the driveway, past the light show."

"Oh. The Mattox place?" The operator's voice got higher, concern coloring her professional tone.

"Yes."

"And your emergency?"

"A man with a broken leg. He was crawling in the snow to get help. And one hand looks nearly frozen. He lost a glove." Lanie tried to speak slowly and clearly, but her words came out at top speed.

While she answered the operator's questions, Lanie opened her trunk and dug through her first aid kit, throwing rejected items onto the floor of the trunk. "Here. I have one of those heat-protective blankets."

"Cover him with it. Don't move him anymore. And hold your hands around his cold one to try to warm it, but don't rub it." There was a crackle over the phone, a second of silence, and then the operator came back on. "The ambulance should be there in ten minutes. I'm taking another call, but I'll stay on the line. I'm here if you need me."

"Okay." Lanie tucked the phone between her ear and shoulder and shook out the blanket.

Kyle lay on his stomach with his head turned to one side.

She covered him and knelt on one edge of the blanket. She couldn't do much to block the wind, but at least she could keep the blanket from blowing away.

"You can't stay with me. You have to pick up April from practice," he said, each word emphatic.

"The ambulance will be here in ten minutes."

"I know you're mad at me, but you can't leave her there with no one to get her." The agitation grew in his tone and he twisted under the blanket, as if trying to roll over, and moaned.

"Quit moving." Her voice came out harsh. She thought of his pain and tried to speak more softly. "There's plenty of time for me to get there. I would never let her feel abandoned."

Kyle sank back down, and his forehead relaxed a fraction. "Thank you."

Lanie pulled off her gloves and took his bare hand in one of hers. It was like holding ice cubes. And he didn't respond, didn't even act like he felt her touch. Not good.

She squeezed her fingers closer against his and wrapped her scarf around their hands. Once it was in place, she slipped her other hand inside, sandwiching his fingers. "I'll bring April to the hospital so we can wait for you."

"Bring her here. She needs dinner. Bedtime . . ."

"But how will you get home?"

"Cab." He squeezed his eyes shut, as if pain had surged through him.

Lanie started to speak, then stopped. Arguing would be useless. Nothing mattered more to Kyle than his daughter.

"Okay. I'll bring her to your house and wait with her. And I'll tell her you'll be fine."

With her eyes, she followed the path he had made through the snow. Had he tripped on something hidden by the drifts? "How did you—" She angled her head toward his leg.

His jaw tightened. "The angel. In the oak."

Lanie peered up. A new decoration had been added to the show, a small angel that didn't change with the music but stayed lit.

"You were putting her up? By yourself?" She tried to judge the height. "In the dark?" The man had no more sense than a first grader.

"For April. She was upset after last night. She thought you'd never spend time with her again and . . ." His voice grew too weak for Lanie to hear.

Guilt exploded in her chest, filling it with lead pellets. She'd hurt that sweet little girl. Even Kyle's injury was partly her fault. Going up a ladder in the dark was idiotic, but he never would have even thought of it if she'd taken the time to talk to April.

And now . . . well, ten minutes had sounded fast, like the ambulance would be right here. But it was taking forever and Kyle looked . . . bad. A little gray.

She wrapped her hands more tightly around his. Small help that was.

Lanie turned toward the cars, full of people watching the light show. No one had blocked the drive tonight; that was good. But if she left Kyle to ask them for help, what could they do?

Nothing.

"You're going to be okay," Lanie said, but even she could hear the doubt in her voice.

The music from the light show paused, switching from one song to the next.

And far in the distance a siren wailed.

She let out a sigh of relief. "That's the ambulance. Can you hear it?"

Kyle gave a short, tight nod.

A few minutes later, two burly, blond paramedics had strapped a collar around his neck, put him on a backboard, and braced his leg. They loaded him in the ambulance, then gave him a shot and wrapped his hand in a heated cloth.

"You coming with us?" one paramedic asked, angling his head toward Lanie.

"I have to pick up his daughter."

The man shrugged in acknowledgment.

"Wait." Kyle fought to sit up, but he was strapped down. Drops of sweat formed on his brow. "Lanie—"

She rushed to the back of the ambulance. "Yes?"

"I didn't want to tell you." His words were slow, as if the painkiller was taking effect. "Derek was cheating on you."

Lanie sucked in a breath.

For a second, Kyle glanced away, unable, or unwilling, to go on. Then he looked back at her. "Seeing two other women." His voice became weaker, harder to hear. "That's why I—"

"That's why you told him not to marry me." Lanie's legs grew weak. She backed away from the ambulance, and its lights swam in front of her.

"He was an idiot," Kyle said more loudly. "He didn't deserve a woman like you."

She took two steps toward him.

But the door clanged shut.

Chapter Nine

The paramedics turned on the lights and siren and drove toward the county road.

Lanie staggered to her car, her brain spinning like a Round Up carnival ride at full speed after the bottom had dropped out.

Kyle hadn't kept silent about Derek because he was heartless. He'd avoided telling her out of pity.

Pity.

Her stomach hardened just thinking of it.

Ahead, the ambulance passed the cars parked to see the light show, then picked up speed. Lanie followed but at a normal pace.

Had Kyle felt anything more than pity?

He didn't deserve a woman like you.

Kyle had sounded earnest, but did that mean what she thought? She forced herself to slow down, to remember the conversation. He'd said Derek was an idiot.

She liked that.

The rest of what he'd said about Derek made perfect sense in retrospect. She and Derek had gone to different universities. Every time she saw him, he had driven to her school, said he didn't want her alone on the highway. She thought he was chivalrous. But now she realized that if she had gone to visit him and hung out with his friends, she might have learned the truth.

Lanie adjusted the blanket to better cover Jellybean and realized something else. Derek had gone on and on about never looking at her phone when a text from a friend popped up. Told her he respected her privacy. That had led her—without his even asking—to do the same with him. If he'd gotten texts from other girls, she never would have known.

Her shoulders sank. She had to be the most gullible woman in the world.

Another mile and Lanie turned onto the highway toward town, now so far behind the ambulance that she no longer heard the siren.

She ought to be glad she'd never married Derek. Be grateful to Kyle for convincing him to break off the engagement. Or be angry.

But mostly she was embarrassed.

All along Kyle had known.

She imagined herself in his position, looking for a time to bring up his role in her past. Not easy. If Kyle had mentioned Derek's infidelity as soon as they'd met, it would have been rude. But waiting made it worse. Like when someone had a piece of lettuce in their teeth.

Only more awkward.

A lot more awkward.

He didn't deserve a woman like you.

She ran the words through her mind again, like a seasoned lawyer weighing every nuance. Was it wishful thinking?

No, Kyle clearly saw the fault as Derek's, not that she was somehow lacking. Maybe he'd seen Derek do the same thing to other women. Lanie shifted her weight in the seat. That didn't make her feel any better.

The real question was this: did Kyle's comment mean that she should be in a relationship with someone more deserving?

Like him?

For a second she pictured a future with Kyle and April, and her heart floated like freshly spun cotton candy, so light it almost defied gravity. From deep inside her, a yearning rose. More than anything, she wanted that future.

Then she remembered the shot—the truly sizable shot—the paramedics had given him. What if Kyle, when not on painkillers, didn't want her in his life—especially after how she'd upset April?

And what if, with taking care of April, there wasn't time to redo the work she had lost? It could all be gone—Kyle, April, and her master's degree.

Every dream she had.

Lanie turned onto the street that led to the Abundance Community Church.

And just as quickly, her mind slid over images of Kyle building a fire for her, Kyle inviting her to make cookies, and Kyle kissing her.

Those images rang true.

As true as the fact that six years ago, he had been a decent man, trying to protect her from a lifetime of pain.

Was it simply a fluke that such a decent man as Kyle shared an apartment with Derek? Lanie raised a hand to where her gold cross necklace used to hang. She had thought God didn't care about her because he had let her go through such pain. But could he have been protecting her too?

A tingling lightness filled her chest.

Maybe Kyle coming into her life wasn't sick cruelty, but part of God's plan.

Lanie pulled into the parking lot. On the church roof, the white steeple shone, illuminated by a small light.

For tonight, she would trust.

Trust that she could take care of April and help her not worry about her dad.

Trust that if she had lost some of her work, she could redo it after the little girl was in bed.

And trust that God had planned good things for her future, a future that might include Kyle.

※

The ER had been slow. Very slow. It was almost midnight when the cab brought Kyle home.

He replayed the nurse's instructions about crutches in his mind and hauled himself out of the cab.

The main house was pitch black, the night silent. The wind that had tortured him as he had lain in the snow was now still.

But at his cottage, all the lights were on.

He'd kept Lanie up late. On top of throwing in her face what had to be the biggest embarrassment of her life. No wonder he botched relationships. He had no tact. He'd blurted out about Derek's cheating with no preamble, no thought that she might not want the paramedics to hear.

One thing was certain, he owed Lanie an apology.

But first he had to get in the house without falling.

He studied the sidewalk. Two inches of snow had fallen after he went to the ER. Someone had shoveled the walk and put out salt.

Not April. Definitely an adult.

Gratitude swirled in his chest.

Thunk. Shuffle. Thunk. Shuffle. Kyle worked his way toward the door, opened it, and let himself inside.

In front of a cozy fire, Jellybean raised her head and gave a soft woof of greeting. In the kitchen, dishes drained by the sink and the counters looked different—straightened.

But he didn't see Lanie.

She had to be somewhere, though. Her laptop was plugged in and open on the kitchen table. The hall light was on, as was the light in April's room. His daughter's bedtime was three hours ago. If she was still awake . . .

Kyle moved down the hall as quietly as he could on crutches and stuck his head inside the door to April's room.

April and Lanie were in the twin bed, both asleep. Lanie slumped against the puffy pink headboard, her head drooped to one side, her hair flowing over the two of them like melted caramel. April was snuggled in close, her mouth slightly open, and Lanie's arms were wrapped tightly around her, as if she wanted to hold her forever.

An ache grew in his chest.

Lanie looked . . . like she belonged with April.

With him.

Pinpricks jabbed his eyes and the back of his throat. He tightened his jaw and swallowed. Lousy pain meds, messing with his emotions.

"Lanie," he said, keeping his voice soft.

No response.

He cleared his throat and tried again. "Lanie."

She stirred, then opened her eyes and jerked her head up. She slid out from under April and tucked the blankets back around her. Then Lanie turned toward him, her eyes wide. "What time is it?" she said in a terse whisper.

"After midnight. The ER was really slow." He shut off the light in April's room.

Lanie was already down the hall.

He stumped his way toward her. "I shouldn't have told you about Derek in front of the paramedics. That was thoughtless of me."

She waved a hand, batting his apology away. "I have to get to my apartment. I just had my computer set up when April wanted me to read more." Lanie's words gushed out, frenzied. She unplugged her laptop and whipped the cord around it several times. "I can't believe I fell asleep."

Kyle ran a hand over his eyes. The pain meds were messing with him again. "But you sent in your last three chapters days ago."

"I did." She grabbed her coat off the back of the couch and shoved one arm into a sleeve.

"Wait," he said.

"Listen, I'm glad you're okay. And I understand that you were in an awkward position with Derek."

She understood, at least a little. He still needed to make sure, though, that she knew she was incredible. "I know it's late," he said, "but can we talk for a minute?"

"I can't." She spoke even faster and her voice rose, like she was about to lose it. "Those chapters I sent were the first round. I have to e-mail my whole thesis—all corrections made—to my advisor by nine in the morning." Then she grabbed her purse and started to put on her boots, her movements frantic. "I spent all day making it perfect. I was about to save it when the power went out. But I can't remember saving anything for the last couple of hours."

For a second, Kyle's chest felt hollow, then guilt rushed in to fill the void. Her computer problems were all his fault. Because of his obsession with Christmas lights.

Granted, the woman should have replaced her battery. And she should save her work more often—a lot more often—but if he hadn't turned around to look at that truck, if he hadn't gone up the ladder in the first place . . .

And then, like the solution to a coding problem, he saw the bigger truth. He couldn't know for certain, but it sure seemed like God had been acting in his life, whether Kyle realized it or not. If Kyle hadn't taken out Lanie's power, she wouldn't have come down the drive. He would have needed to crawl all the way to the main house, and he might not have made it. And how likely was it that the ladder would fly toward the power line? Or that she would actually see him in the snow? In the dark?

And—

He wobbled and grabbed the edge of the couch.

And how likely was it that such an amazing woman would be dropped right into his life?

Even when she had offered to pick up April at church, Lanie had known how much work she had to do, and she hadn't said a word.

She'd willingly sacrificed her whole evening—hours of her time—to help April, to help him. She was giving, caring. Not at all like Tiffany.

And even when he told her about Derek—with about as much finesse as a caveman's club, when she had to be hurt and angry with Derek and with him—she had gone over and beyond, taking the trouble to put salt on his sidewalk.

He needed to tell her how much that meant to him.

As fast as he could, Kyle clomped to the kitchen, then laid his hand on her arm. "Hey—"

She spun toward him, her face pale, eyes anxious. As much as he wanted to talk with her, he had to let her get her thesis turned in first.

"Uh," he mumbled, "why don't you check while you're here? If your file is okay, wouldn't you rather know sooner?"

She gave a single nod, slipped off her coat, and plugged her laptop back in.

He sat at the table beside her. She typed with jerky movements, then looked up, every muscle in her face tight. "It's gone. At least two hours of work. Those really good pages I wrote at the end. I don't know if I can write them again and—"

"What about the temp file?"

Her eyebrows drew together. "What?"

His heart picked up speed and he looked her straight in the eye. "Let me help you."

He could find her file.

And find a way to be the man she deserved.

Chapter Ten

"Can you do the search really fast?" Lanie slid the computer toward Kyle but didn't let go of the edge. "If it's not there, I'll have to redo all those changes and the new pages..." She didn't want to even think about how much work it would be.

"I'll find it." He pulled the laptop in front of him.

"Are you sure?"

"Lanie, this is what I do. Trust me." He sounded a little insulted.

She bit her lip, moved to stand behind him, and shifted her weight back and forth from one foot to the other.

Kyle pulled up a window she'd never seen, and though the fingers of his right hand looked a bit pink, he typed rapidly, as if for him—even after his hand had been so cold, even on pain meds—the search was routine.

Maybe he would find her file. That would be wonderful. But what was that look he'd given her? He'd said he wanted to talk and then she told him how she lost her file and he'd looked . . . well, guilty.

She tried to tell herself she was being paranoid, but nerves pricked their way up her throat like claws.

Kyle double-clicked loudly. "Here," he said. "What about this?"

She bent forward. It was her file, but she couldn't tell how recent. "Scroll down, almost to the end."

He touched the trackpad and the pages flew by.

Then he stopped and she read the page.

Her pulse quickened. That paragraph at the bottom was the transition she'd written to start her insightful pages. Was the rest of it there? She sat back down in the chair to his right and nodded toward the laptop. "May I?"

Kyle slid the computer toward her.

She scrolled through page after page.

Her last formatting changes had been made. The last spelling errors she'd found had been fixed. And her two insightful pages—every word she'd slaved over—were there.

Her breath came out in a whoosh. "This is it—everything, right before the power went out."

"Save it," he said and waved his hands, urging her to hurry.

With trembling fingers, she named the file and saved it. Then she exhaled and slumped against the chair. "Thank you, Kyle. You're a lifesaver."

A flush rose in his cheeks. "It's the least I can do." He sounded embarrassed. "After—"

"I couldn't leave you lying out there in the snow."

"You did way more than that. In spite of what I said in front of the paramedics, you took care of April, even when it meant you might not graduate. You even shoveled the sidewalk and put out salt so I wouldn't fall on my crutches. But that's not what I meant."

She looked at him and nerves clawed at her throat again. She wasn't being paranoid. He sounded guilty.

"I took out your power. When I fell. The ladder hit the electrical line." His words came out wooden, like he couldn't quite believe what he'd done.

Her mouth dropped open, and she closed it and swallowed. "You—you could have been electrocuted." Clearly, the man needed someone to watch over him.

He shifted in his chair. "Let me connect my Wi-Fi and you can e-mail your file." He spoke quickly, as if he didn't want to dwell on his fall.

She slid the laptop back to him and Kyle typed rapidly.

Eager to end the ordeal of her thesis, she reached toward the computer, but he raised his head with an odd expression on his face. "I think—" His speech slowed and became more deliberate. "Before I let you send your file, I need some assurances from you."

Lanie scooted back in her chair. What on earth was he talking about?

"If you get your master's, you're hoping to find a job somewhere else, right?"

"St. Louis," Lanie said.

"If I let you use my Internet, you're going to have to promise to spend Christmas with April and me." He paused, his eyes glued to her. "The pageant, the big meal, even"—he leaned forward—"even Christmas morning."

Lanie inhaled sharply. Her heart pounded and the air in the room changed, as if some new element had been added, one that made her warm and tingly and unable to speak. She wanted it all. Wanted to sit up front in church with Kyle to see April in the pageant. Wanted to share the holiday meal with people she cared about. Wanted to watch April's face as she opened presents, including the special box of colored pencils Lanie had ordered for her.

Kyle moved back, hunched over the laptop, and clicked a few keys, his eyes on the screen. "I'm sorry. That wasn't fair. You . . . you can use the Internet. It's not conditional." The warmth had left his tone. "I just wanted you to be part of—"

"Wait," she said. She'd taken too long to speak and he'd misunderstood. She placed her hand on his arm. "Christmas with you and April would be wonderful."

Kyle's eyes met hers, and he reached to squeeze her hand. "Good." He scooted the laptop in front of her. "You, uh, better send your file."

Lanie typed in her e-mail password and sent her thesis to her advisor. Then she moved the cursor over to see her Sent e-mail, just to make sure that she hadn't gotten so distracted by Kyle that she'd somehow messed it up.

But there it was, turned in. She let out a long sigh.

"If we spend Christmas together, it will give me plenty of time." Kyle's voice was rich with promise.

"Time for what?" She turned to face him.

He shifted his chair nearer and placed his hand on her upper arm. "To convince you to stay here."

Electricity shot through her body, and she drew in a quick breath.

His eyes met hers and grew darker.

"I think it's where we're meant to be." He slid his fingers up her arm and buried them in the hair at the nape of her neck, then drew her face toward his. "In Abundance. Together."

Lanie's mouth grew dry and warmth built in her chest. She ran her tongue over her lips and leaned toward him.

"Daddy!"

Lanie jolted back in her seat.

April raced toward them and leaped into Kyle's arms. "You're home."

Kyle held April close and stared over her shoulder at Lanie, the kiss he'd been about to give her still in his eyes.

The kiss she still wanted.

But she could wait. Her heart already felt like it might burst at the tender sight of April in his arms. And at thoughts of the future.

"I should go to my apartment. It's after midnight." Lanie grabbed her things and walked to the door, then looked back at Kyle. "But Christmas sounds perfect."

The perfect time to collect that kiss.

༒

"Got it in focus?" Lanie slid closer on the pew.

Kyle let his gaze rest on her face, then adjusted the tripod and rechecked the viewfinder of the video camera. "All set." He had a full view of the stage and could film April's pageant without moving the camera. "Thanks again for driving us. Here and earlier, so I could get the cast put on."

Lanie gave a no-big-deal shrug.

Ordinarily, he hated being dependent, unable to drive. But if it meant more time with Lanie, he was more than willing to adjust. He'd take all the time in the world to gaze at her beautiful face and silky hair, to glance at the bright-blue dress that hugged her soft curves.

He drew in a deep breath. Her coconut fragrance mingled with the scent of the evergreen boughs that lined the sanctuary windowsills. "You're, uh, you're sure Jellybean is okay alone at your apartment?"

"Turns out my landlord is actually a big softie. He's checking on her."

The organ prelude began, and the minister walked to the center of the stage. After a brief welcome for visitors and an opening prayer, he stepped aside and the director introduced the pageant. Kyle turned on the video camera. Soon he found himself drawn in, listening to the children act out the story of the birth of Jesus. Why had he resisted April being in the pageant? It was a great experience. And being an angel was perfect. No need to speak during her first time on stage. All she had to do was stand there and be beautiful, wearing the wings Lanie had made. He looked to the side of the stage, searching for April.

And then, there she was, climbing on a riser off to the left, near the shepherds—not simply one of the angels, but the main angel, the one front and center.

Kyle double-checked the video camera.

"Look. They put the cutest in front," Lanie whispered.

April glanced at the director, then moved toward a microphone.

Kyle shot Lanie a nervous look. April hadn't said she had a speaking part, hadn't practiced with him at all.

"Fear not." Her voice wavered. No one could hear her past the third row back. He should have told the director she was shy.

The director cupped a hand near her ear.

April moved closer to the mic, and her voice grew stronger, along with her confidence. "For, behold, I bring you good tidings of great joy, which shall be to all people."

Kyle nudged Lanie. Did she see how great April was doing? When had she learned the verses from the second chapter of Luke?

"For unto you is born this day in the city of David a Savior, which is Christ the Lord." Her words rang out, each enunciated clearly, and her young voice sounded so sweet that it had to stir every heart in the audience. "And this shall be a sign unto you; ye shall find the babe wrapped in swaddling clothes, lying in a manger."

Kyle wiped his eyes.

Lanie nudged him. She was silently clapping, her eyes on April.

Kyle quickly held two thumbs up high.

The organ played softly, and the other angels stepped forward and joined April. "Glory to God in the highest, and on earth peace, good will toward men," they said, almost in unison, then left the stage.

The shepherds found Jesus, the wise men came from the east, and Mary treasured up all these things in her heart. But Kyle had trouble focusing. His girl was a star.

Soon the pageant was over and the congregation stood to sing "Joy to the World." The director released the children, and April bounded toward them.

"You were amazing," Kyle said. He squeezed her close, careful not to crush her wings.

Her eyes sparkled. "Miss Hamlin says I'm a natural, says some of the best actors in the world are shy when they're not on stage."

She sounded so grown-up that Kyle stared.

"Becky's right," Lanie said, her eyes as bright as April's. "And it was a fabulous pageant."

Kyle swallowed hard. God had blessed him with so much.

He made his way to the director and thanked her. Three times. Then he clomped toward the door. Twice he was stopped by members of the congregation who told him that April was the star of the whole show. They were right.

At the front door, where Lanie brought her car, he stowed his crutches in the back, then hopped to the front and sank into the seat. He didn't call Tiffany often, since she had made it clear she didn't want to be involved, but tomorrow he would call so he could tell her what an incredible job April had done. And he would upload a copy of the video for her.

Lanie drove through town into an area Kyle didn't know.

"Where are we going?" April asked.

"Jellybean and I have been staying at my apartment until the power is back on at the farmhouse." Lanie turned into the parking lot of a three-story brick building. "Come inside."

She led them in the entrance, opened the door of her first-floor unit, and pointed April toward the kitchen, toward the whelping box Kyle remembered seeing at his aunt and uncle's.

April took one slow step, then squealed. "Puppies!" She dashed toward the box.

"I think they're asleep," Lanie whispered, and she laid a hand on April's shoulder. "And Jellybean probably doesn't want us to pet them yet. They were born yesterday, while you were practicing and having your cast party."

April nodded but kept her eyes on the puppies.

Kyle drew nearer. In the box, small furry bodies snuggled against Jellybean, some flopped across the others. He counted six. As he looked at each pup in turn, more of his objections to a dog melted.

April gazed up at him, her eyes round. "Can we have one, Daddy, pleeeeeeeease?"

A tiny shred of common sense kept him silent. Much as he wanted a dog, his eight-hour work days were too long to leave a puppy inside. He worked straight through lunch so he could leave early to pick April up.

But how could he resist the little ears, the tiny noses, the miniature furry paws, and April's huge, pleading eyes?

"You know," Lanie said. "I'm getting one. I asked your aunt yesterday when I texted her photos. Maybe this little fellow right here." She pointed to a puppy who was darker than the others, almost black. "You could come visit him anytime you wanted."

Kyle's breath caught.

"But—" April tilted her head. "I thought you were moving."

"Well, I am moving to a new apartment, one that allows pets. But I've decided to stay right here in Abundance, at least for a year." Her tone was nonchalant, but she gazed at Kyle as if seeking reassurance.

"Yaaaaaaaaay!" April yelled so loudly that his ears rang, then she leaped to her feet and gave Lanie a huge hug.

Suddenly woken, one of the puppies let out a soft mewl.

In an instant, April knelt back down beside them, oblivious to the rest of the world.

Kyle turned to Lanie, his chest tight with emotion. "You're staying?"

She looked at the puppies and her hair fell forward, hiding her face. "I can always apply for jobs in St. Louis next year." Her tone—nervous and embarrassed—confused him.

Kyle leaned his hips against the counter. Then he set his crutches to the side and reached over to take Lanie's hands in his. "Hey, come here." He gently pulled her to face him.

She looked up at him and he struggled for a breath. The woman was so beautiful he could barely function, but he had to figure out what was going on, had to ease the tension around her eyes. "I'm really glad you'll be here. I know we need time to get to know each other better, but I think we belong together."

"You said that the other night." She gestured to his cast. "But later I wondered if it might have been the painkillers talking."

Kyle let go of her fingers and slid his hands around her waist. "No way."

Her face relaxed, and a hint of a smile teased the corners of her lips.

Then she stepped closer, until the sweet scent of coconut surrounded him.

His breath grew shallow. "It wasn't the painkillers." His voice came out husky. "It was me, realizing I love you."

She blinked rapidly and her lips parted. The corners of her mouth tipped up bit by bit. "You do?"

His throat grew dry and he nodded.

She gazed at him, her eyes shining, then reached her arms around his neck until her mouth was only inches from his. "I love you too."

Her words were choked with emotion, barely more than a whisper, but they resonated in his ears and in his heart and in the very marrow of his bones.

His heart thudded and he drew her close, until her body melted into his.

Heat exploded in his chest and swirled through him. He lowered his lips to hers.

This woman—this kind and beautiful and giving woman—was someone he could trust for the rest of his days.

And this woman loved him.

Epilogue

One year later

"Look." Megan pointed out the car window.

Lanie glanced up from the road. A small sign peeped above the deep piles of snow and proclaimed "You're almost to the Phillips-Mattox wedding!"

A pair of gold, linked wedding bands adorned one top corner of the sign, and two silver bells had been painted in the other corner. Tiny bits of glitter sparkled in the bright sunlight on the sign's lettering.

She turned to her sister and felt a smile spread across her face, a smile that probably looked sappy. She couldn't help it. Today was the day she and Kyle had been waiting for. Their wedding day.

The words sent a tingle through her chest. Just a few more hours to wait.

In the backseat, her nephews squirmed and elbowed each other, jockeying for possession of the fold-down center armrest. Except for the fact that both Wyatt and Anthony had dark hair, watching them was like seeing herself and Megan two decades ago.

"Did April really paint that sign?" Anthony, five, sounded skeptical.

"No way," Wyatt said with a snort. "She's only six."

Lanie bit back a chuckle. Seven-year-old Wyatt was full of himself, just like Megan had been. And still was.

"Not the lettering, but she did the rings and the bells," Lanie said. Megan's boys weren't quite sure what to make of April. Except around adults she'd never met, the girl's shyness had disappeared. With two boys, one a year older and one a year younger, she was more than comfortable telling them what to do.

Lanie rounded a curve and spotted Megan's husband pulling up one of the signs for the Mattox Christmas light show. He positioned a second, new sign and hammered it in place for today's event. Decorated much like the first sign with rings and bells, it said, "Please park on this side. Do not block the sleigh."

"I can't believe you're leaving from your wedding in a horse-drawn sleigh," Megan said.

"I can't either." Lanie's heart grew warm just thinking about it. "It was Kyle's idea. The sleigh will take us right to the bed and breakfast for our honeymoon."

"I knew that man had potential." Megan's tone made it clear that if Lanie wanted to mention how brilliant her older sister was, now would be the time.

Lanie rolled her eyes but didn't say a word. Instead she breathed a silent prayer of thanks.

She'd thought Kyle was a jerk.

Wrong.

He was the man of her dreams.

And she'd thought God didn't love her.

Wrong again.

God—that same God she thought didn't care—had shown her again and again over the past year that he did.

Two hours later, in Kelly and Rich's bedroom, her dressing room for the day, Lanie smoothed a lock of April's hair under the girl's headband and adjusted one of the red rosebuds that adorned it.

April studied her reflection in a standing oval mirror. She patted the full skirt of her dress, a dark green satin scattered with tiny white bows. Then she turned to face Lanie. Her soft, little hand settled on Lanie's arm, as if she were afraid to touch the white gown. "I love you," she said, her words as soft as dandelion fluff.

A lump grew in the back of Lanie's throat, and she bent down and pulled April close. Lanie had known so many sweet children in the classroom, but April was different, like she'd been born to fill a space in Lanie's heart. "I love you, too, cutie pie," she whispered.

And then Rich Mattox began playing Pachelbel's "Canon in D Major" on the baby grand.

"Time to go." Megan beckoned April over and handed her a basket of red rose petals.

April picked up a handful, let them fall through her fingers back into the basket, and looked up at Lanie, her eyes shining, her whole face alight.

Lanie blinked back tears. This sweet girl, so eager to have her be family.

"No crying," Megan waved a finger at Lanie, scolding her like an old-time schoolmarm.

"You're right," April said to Lanie. "She is bossy."

Lanie laughed. Oh, she was going to love having April around all the time.

Megan folded her arms across her chest and gave a tight frown that could do a schoolmarm proud. But her eyes sparkled. "I'm only bossy when it's needed. Now scoot. The music's started."

April gave a mischievous smile and walked out slowly, just like they had practiced.

"All right, I'm next," Megan said. She ran a hand over her hips, smoothing her forest-green sheath, and picked up a nosegay of red and white roses.

"You look beautiful," Lanie said. All that agonizing over dresses had been worth it. The color was perfect with Megan's dark hair and green eyes.

"And you"—Megan's voice cracked—"look stunning."

Lanie pulled her into a hug. Megan might be bossy, but she was the best sister ever.

Megan gave Lanie's shoulders a final squeeze and stepped toward the door.

Alone, Lanie drew in a deep breath and checked her reflection. A simple white satin sheath that hit midcalf. High white satin heels, each adorned with one satin rosebud. Her hair done up with a few loose tendrils falling on her shoulders. She rubbed a spot on her cheek, repairing the smudge from a tear.

Then she raised one hand to her collarbone, to her cross necklace. She'd dug it out of the trash, where it had sat next to a single used tissue, and taken it to the jewelers to have it cleaned. She rubbed her thumb over it. How could she have thrown it away?

Never again—which is why now she wore it all the time. Not as a good-luck charm, but as a reminder that God's love was constant, even when she couldn't understand it, even when bad things happened.

This day, this wedding, was proof to her that God had loved her through it all. Emotion welled in her chest. Through all the pain and the hurt, God had been watching over her. And she hadn't even known it.

The music segued into "The Wedding March," and Lanie's breath caught. Time to marry a man who'd protected her before he even knew her.

God's blessings were amazing.

She gathered up a cascade of red roses, breathed in their fragrance, and moved into the hall.

Jellybean wandered toward her. Lanie's puppy, Hershey, followed right behind, wearing Kyle's antler cap.

Lanie stifled a giggle.

Then she rounded the corner into the living room. Kyle stood near the fireplace, so handsome in his black tux that for a second, she couldn't get a breath.

His eyes met hers, and emotion flooded her heart until her hands shook.

She moved toward Kyle and the minister, barely seeing the people she passed—friends from work, Kelly and her daughter Jill and her family, Megan and Mark and the boys. They were all a peripheral haze. Lanie's eyes stayed on Kyle.

At last she stood facing him. His mouth tipped up in a wide smile, and his dark brown eyes crinkled around the edges, filled with tenderness. He enclosed her shaking hands in his and held them.

Warmth wrapped around her and her trembling stilled. Lanie gazed up at him, ready to promise her love.

To a man she could trust.

Forever.

A NOTE FROM SALLY

Dear Reader,

Thank you for reading *Christmas in Abundance*. I had so much fun with this story! I hope it was fun for you as well.

The inspiration for this novella was very close to home. When our children were young, my husband and I often took them to see a wonderful Christmas light show near our house. That light show, however, had its own FM frequency, so we listened to the music on the radio of our trusty minivan. One fall, as I drove home from a writer's conference, I began to think of a story about a single dad running a light show and blasting a whole neighborhood with the same songs again and again. Three years later that idea resurfaced and I wrote *Christmas in Abundance*.

If you enjoyed this story, please visit my website at www.sallybayless.com to learn about upcoming releases.

And now may God bless you, and may you know—every day—how incredibly huge his love is for you.

Sally Bayless

ABOUT THE AUTHOR

Sally Bayless was born and raised in the Missouri Ozarks and now lives in the beautiful hills of Appalachian Ohio with her husband and two teenage children. When not working on her next book, she enjoys watching BBC television with her husband, doing Bible studies, swimming, baking, and shopping for cute shoes.

Christmas in Abundance is Sally's debut publication. Her next release, due out in 2016, is a full-length contemporary romance novel and is also set in Abundance, Missouri.

ACKNOWLEDGMENTS

I am incredibly grateful to the many people who have helped me in writing this story.

Robert A. Holm, Jr., D.O. FACEP, graciously reviewed sections dealing with emergency medical care. Ann Graber Flanagin, Theresa Reinkemeyer, and Derrick Gwinner of the Columbia Public Schools answered questions related to teaching in Missouri. Their help was wonderful. Any errors that slipped in are mine.

My story is stronger, my characters deeper, and innumerable errors are corrected thanks to my wonderful critique partners, authors Susan Anne Mason and Tammy Doherty, and my fabulous beta readers, Carrie Saunders, Carolyn Smith, Diana West, Jan LeBar, Jona Moberg, Kristina Gerig, Leisa Ostermann, and Stephanie Smith.

Sally Bradley was my developmental editor. Amy K. Maddox of The Blue Pencil did the copy edits. I cannot say enough good things about either of them. This story would not be what it is today without their efforts.

Thanks to Emily Reynolds for everything she taught me about writing and for her encouragement.

And special thanks to my dear friend Tammy Atkins, who passed away in 2006. Tammy believed in my writing before I did.

Thanks to American Christian Fiction Writers and Romance Writers of America for years of education and invaluable resources. To Susan May Warren, Rachel Hauck, and the team at My Book Therapy for their amazing teaching. And to the members of Writing GIAM who keep me moving toward my goals.

I wrote this story while participating in National Novel Writing Month 2014. Although I've rarely shared rough drafts, I let my husband, Dave, read the first few chapters. Each evening afterward, he encouraged me, asked for the next chapter, and laughed in the right places. As always, his support was amazing.

Michael, thank you for your tech skills. Every writer needs a patient son majoring in computer engineering. Laurel, thank you for your comments on the manuscript. If your language skills are this sharp at age fifteen, I cannot wait to see what they are like after college. And thanks to both of you for putting up with a mom who's a writer. At least this book wasn't a romantic suspense like some of my stories. Not once while writing it did I mention methods of murder at the dinner table.

And finally, thank you, God, for the blessings and love you pour over me and for bringing me closer to you on this journey.

Made in the USA
Charleston, SC
17 September 2015